A STOLEN MOMENT

"They are odd little plants, aren't they?" Lord Wakefield said, moving away.

Meg sat back on his jacket. "I almost expect to see a fairy dancing beside them."

She couldn't tell if his reaction was a half-laugh or a sniff of censure. "I think a beetle or some winged insect would be far more likely. How did your sketches turn out?"

She held them up and he crouched down again, studying the drawings. "Very realistic, very detailed."

He was so very close, nearly touching her shoulder, his cheek only inches from hers. Meg's heart pounded unexplainably as he lifted her hand and turned it over, intertwining his fingers with hers. He raised it to his mouth and touched the back of her hand with his lips, then turned it over and kissed her palm.

Deep within her, Meg felt a warmth invade her innermost being, a series of tingles dance along her nerves. She dared not move, dared not breathe.

With his thumb, Wakefield caressed her jaw, then turned her chin toward him and very slowly, very softly touched her lips with his.

"Miss Hayward, you have a most unusual effect on me."

BOOK YOUR PLACE ON OUR WEBSITE AND MAKE THE READING CONNECTION!

We've created a customized website just for our very special readers, where you can get the inside scoop on everything that's going on with Zebra, Pinnacle and Kensington books.

When you come online, you'll have the exciting opportunity to:

- View covers of upcoming books
- Read sample chapters
- Learn about our future publishing schedule (listed by publication month *and author*)
- Find out when your favorite authors will be visiting a city near you
- Search for and order backlist books from our online catalog
- Check out author bios and background information
- Send e-mail to your favorite authors
- Meet the Kensington staff online
- Join us in weekly chats with authors, readers and other guests
- Get writing guidelines
- AND MUCH MORE!

**Visit our website at
http://www.kensingtonbooks.com**

THE FONTAINEBLEAU FAN

Victoria Hinshaw

ZEBRA BOOKS
Kensington Publishing Corp.
http://www.kensingtonbooks.com

One

Meg Hayward hugged the velvet pouch and stared at the jumble of people, horses, and vehicles crowding the noisy London street. In all her twenty-one years in rural Sussex, she had never experienced so much boisterous confusion. Livy, her nineteen-year-old sister, shared the shabby hackney and peered at the chaos with a look of astonishment. Meg gave a little shiver at the tumult. The duty that had seemed so simple and logical two days earlier now loomed before her, fraught with unanticipated obstacles.

But for the moment, she could not look away from the disorderly scene. No more than a few feet away, a plump woman wrapped in black shawls and holding a basket of onions shrilled incomprehensible grievances at a little fellow in a tall, crooked hat. A cacophony of vendors' shouts merged with the jangle of straining harnesses as snorting horses dragged barrel-laden wagons past piles of cabbages and potatoes in the open market. A pink-rouged dandy cracked his whip over the bony nag pulling a battered old barouche packed with a bevy of satin-clad women.

"What are they doing?" Livy asked, open-mouthed

as she watched the strumpets beckon with crimson-dyed ostrich feathers to passersby.

"I suspect we do not want to know." Meg gripped the pouch and sank back against the dusty cushions. She closed her eyes for a moment and felt the lurching of the hackney as it turned a corner. She simply had to keep her composure.

"Wakefield House, miss," the driver called.

The magnificent mansion sat on a serene tree-lined square, a world away from the teeming streets they had just left, and the very epitome of aristocratic grandeur. Meg took Livy's arm as they climbed out of the carriage. Livy's right leg was shorter and weaker than her left, with the toe turned in and twisted. It gave her a decided limp. Livy bravely boasted she had both a crooked gait and a poetic soul in common with Lord Byron.

The driver set their baggage on the steps, tipped his hat, and drove off, leaving them alone.

Meg swallowed against the tightness in her throat, lifted the heavy brass knocker, and banged it sharply. With its deep timbre, an ominous surge of apprehension hit the pit of her stomach, and her heart pounded a quick cadence.

"Meggy, I'm frightened," Livy whispered.

"Of what, you silly goose?" Meg tried for a confident tone, hiding the tremor in her hands by clutching her pouch even closer. All her assurances to Aunt Alice and Aunt Regina rang hollow.

The massive door swung open on silent hinges. A black-clad butler stared down at them with blank gray eyes. "Yes?" he said, imbuing that single syllable with an hauteur that challenged their right to obtrude upon his time.

Meg tucked a stray golden curl into her bonnet and sought a tone of equal consequence. "I am Margaret Hayward of Cawthorn Manor in Sussex. I wish to speak with Lord Wakefield on an important matter."

"Is his lordship expecting you?" His manner indicated he knew the answer.

"No, he is not."

"Is his lordship acquainted with you?"

"No, he is not," she repeated with all the dignity she could muster.

"His lordship is engaged and cannot be disturbed."

Meg slipped her arm through Livy's and pushed past the startled man into a marble-floored hall. She and Livy settled themselves upon a decorative bench beneath the magnificent stairway.

"Please inform the earl that we await his convenience. You might add we wish to discuss the Fontainebleau fan."

The butler paused, then with a look of patronizing distaste set their meager baggage barely inside the door. With the curtest possible nod, he disappeared through a gilded doorway.

"Meggy, he does not approve, I can tell," Livy whispered.

"For an instant, I thought he might shove us back and slam the door in our faces. Why anyone would employ such a rude fellow is beyond me. I suppose he will let us sit for quite a time."

During the long silence, Meg's heartbeat calmed a little. When she felt composed once more, she gripped the velvet pouch and circled the hall. "Very elegant." She looked upward at the classical frieze above the entrance. "Robert Adam's work, without doubt, for the proportions are impeccable."

She ran her finger along a porphyry table and carefully studied the marble Venus in a curved alcove on one side of the double stairway. The statue's face was delicately beautiful, her stance graceful, one perfect breast bared by her superbly carved robe.

Curious, Meg went to the identical spot on the other side of the stairway. Here stood a majestic Apollo adorned with nothing but a marble drape over one arm. His naked manhood was sculpted in exquisite detail, and due to the statue's position on a golden pedestal, Meg found its most interesting feature to be precisely at eye level.

Abruptly she turned to her sister, but Livy had already noticed the statue and scurried over for a better view.

"I rather suppose the original ancient statue was modeled from life," Meg said.

Livy nodded, wide-eyed. "Seems an awkward thing."

"Somehow quite defenseless."

"You have precisely one minute to explain what you want, Miss Hayward." The deep voice echoed from the other side of the hall.

Meg whirled, drawing a deep breath. She knew her face was flaming. Her embarrassment at being found gawking at the statue changed into surprise. She had expected a much older man, not a specimen every bit as young and virile as the statue, albeit fully clothed.

"Lord Wakefield," she gulped. "Good afternoon. I believe you purchased a fan last month in Sussex?"

"I did." Irritation rippled from his tall frame. His face would have been handsome, Meg thought, if not distorted by arrogant disdain. Obviously he considered

Livy and her less worthy of his attention than a pair of rodents.

"By accident," she continued, "the fan you purchased was not the original antique as represented by Monsieur LeClerque."

She paused, expecting him to respond, but he simply stared at her with angrily glittering eyes.

"I am very sorry, my lord, but your fan is a copy."

"LeClerque said that fan once belonged to Madame de Pompadour." His voice tensed, rising in fury. "Are you telling me I bought a fake?"

She nodded, trying to smile. "I want to—"

"I should have known that devil of a villainous frog was a cheat."

"Lord Wakefield," Meg began. "I have brought—"

He cut her off with an impatient wave of a hand. "How do you know what I have is not genuine?"

"Because I painted it myself."

"Ah! So you are in league with that thief!" He glared past Meg. "Who is she?"

"This is my sister, Miss Olivia Hayward."

"What was her role in this swindle?"

"Why, none at all."

Livy differed immediately. "I assisted by preparing the sticks and gluing on the leaves."

Livy's refusal to be intimidated stiffened Meg's own resolve. "When we realized the mistake, we immediately set off—"

"Mistake!" he thundered. *"Crime* is the correct term."

"My lord." Meg softened her voice, trying to force him to listen. "We are just off the coach from Bexhill. We have not even engaged lodgings as yet. We came immediately to explain."

"I am in no mood for absurd excuses!"

"My lord, I have brought you the real Fontainebleau fan." She held the velvet pouch up in the air.

He strode toward her and reached for the pouch, but she snatched it back against her body. "No, my lord. I won't give it to you until you return the other fan, my copy."

"What? Why do you want that?"

"It belongs to me. When I have it in my possession, you may have this one."

He gave a disgusted sigh. "I do not often use fans myself, Miss Hayward. I presented it as a gift."

To his mistress, she supposed. A fitting favor for a fancy woman. "Then we will have to go get it."

"I gave it to my grandmama, the dowager countess. She lives in Berkshire, a drive of several hours."

Meg was silent for a moment. Could she trust him to destroy the copy? No! She had to be positive it would never fall accidentally into another's hands. She summoned her most insistent voice. "I must have that fan, my lord."

Meg conjured up a look of strict tenacity, or at least the closest she could come to severity while her heart pounded so swiftly. The Earl of Wakefield was impressive in a most unexpected way. Even she could recognize the first rank of elegance in his attire, his bearing, and his shrewd look. Yet she was surprised when he broke into a smile of satirical condescension.

"If you are to have the fan, you will have to continue your journey."

"So it would seem, my lord."

"I suppose there is no reason I cannot go to Berkshire this afternoon instead of tomorrow. My coach will leave for Wakefield Hall within the hour."

* * *

"Why did you not give him the real fan, Meg?" Livy asked.

Meg reclined against the fine squabs of the earl's traveling coach and shook her head. "I suppose I should have handed him the pouch, turned around, and marched right out of his house." She caressed the sumptuous upholstery. She had been a small child the last time she had ridden in such luxury. "But then we would be staying in some miserable coaching inn rather than heading out of town in a quite different style from the way we arrived."

Livy frowned, and even to Meg, her attempt at making a joke fell flat. "I lost my temper. His attitude was so contemptuous, I could not bear it."

"But where in Berkshire is his house? And what will happen when we get there?" Livy asked.

"We will not hear Lord High-and-Haughty's plans while he is out there on horseback, will we?"

"What if he is taking us to some lonely place and he . . . he . . ."

"From the look of his town house and his coach, his lordship can afford the finest of everything. I doubt that ravishing a pair of country nobodies would suit his taste."

Livy shivered. "I hope you are right. But how will we get home?"

Meg unfolded a thick cashmere lap robe and arranged it over their legs, burying her hands in its soft folds. "We will demand he return us to London. Then we will take the post, as planned."

"Aunt Alice and the girls will worry about us if we are not back tomorrow."

"I know." Meg patted Livy's hand. "They always fear the worst, but we can't help that. Perhaps we could be home by nightfall."

"I do hope so."

"Imagine the earl reacting so violently to a simple mistake. Not that Gaston wasn't trying to cheat him."

"You mean he sold your fan to Lord Wakefield on purpose?"

"Gaston probably intended to sell all of them as antiques. I should have surmised as much when he gave me the original to copy."

"Then Lord Wakefield was right! It was not a mistake at all."

"I am sure Gaston had only our best interests at heart. He wanted a better price for us. And for himself."

"That was dishonest."

"I know. But since meeting his lordship, I regret ever trying to make amends."

"If Gaston sold all the fans we made as originals, we would have enough money to repair the roof," Livy mused.

"Livy, do not even think of it! Anyway, I already did away with the other fans."

"No, how could you? Oh, I suppose you were right, but it would be so nice to have a bit of extra money."

"Indeed it would." Meg closed her eyes for a second and felt the weariness wash over her. They had started from Sussex very early that morning and now the setting sun tinted the spring landscape with an ethereal golden glow. As the coach rounded a curve, she caught a glimpse of Lord Wakefield ahead, mounted on a magnificent dapple gray.

She never once speculated he might be angry when

she offered him the antique fan, much less that he
would accuse her of villainy. How foolish she was,
with her fantasies that he would be grateful to her.
Instead, he was furious.

Despite her reassurances to Livy, Meg knew her
own reaction to Lord Wakefield's arrogance had
dumped them both into a real bumblebroth. They never
should have come. Her sister looked pale, her eyes
blank. How could she have been so foolish as to in-
volve Livy, poor, fragile, crippled Livy? All for a
worthless fan.

No, actually the fan was entirely incidental. They
were here in this coach because she had refused to
comply with the demands of that supercilious beast
out there on his fancy desert horse. She had made the
return of her fan a matter of honor. It was her own
fault.

As the carriage rolled on through the twilight, Meg's
thoughts centered entirely on Lord Wakefield. There
was such a disconcerting irony to the earl, such extreme incongruity between his strikingly handsome
looks and his despicable disposition. She doubted he
would have an ounce of compassion in his soul.

When the coach came to a stop, Meg guessed they
had been traveling for almost three hours without a
stop. A footman opened the door of the coach. "Wakefield Hall," he said in a tone that made Meg wonder
if they were expected to kiss the ground.

By the light pouring from the open doorway, a liv-
eried footman led them up a flight of steps, and she
looked around in awe.

The chamber's stone walls were hung with spears
and swords arranged in decorative circles. Banners in
rich red and blue hung overhead from the shadowy

oaken beams far above them. Suits of armor flanked a gigantic fireplace, and the room was lit by several tall iron candelabra holding dozens of flickering candles.

"This is some sort of castle," Meg whispered to her speechless sister.

In the center of the room, Lord Wakefield handed his hat to a footman while the butler removed his multicaped greatcoat. Sound in the cavernous room echoed eerily, and Meg could make out only a word or two from where she and Livy stood together near the door.

The earl's hair was windblown, though he was very much in command as he walked toward the massive fire. He warmed his hands, silhouetted against the flames, as he spoke to his servants. Meg tried to suppress the tremor of fear that shook her. He had an authoritative presence, compelling in his mastery.

If he intended some midnight confrontation with his grandmother, Meg wished he would get on with it instead of leaving them at the door as if they were beggars.

"This way, miss." A woman in black, probably a housekeeper, set off for the staircase.

Meg hesitated, looking at the footman who held their bags, then at Lord Wakefield.

The earl met her eyes across the chamber. Meg did not move to follow the housekeeper.

As Meg hoped, Lord Wakefield walked toward them.

"You have a most impressive collection of weaponry," she said when he came near.

"If attacked by a bevy of knights, we are well supplied." He raised one eyebrow in an amusedly sardonic expression.

"How very reassuring." Meg tried her very best to match his inflection. "Now that we are here, my lord, do you have my fan?"

"The countess has long been abed, Miss Hayward. If you will follow Mrs. Leland, you may refresh yourselves and rest until morning."

Meg frowned. "I hoped to have the matter settled tonight."

"I assure you the countess would not take kindly to being awakened at this hour."

"Your room is this way," the housekeeper said.

"Then we shall wish you good night," Meg said with what she hoped was enough grace and refinement to hide her true wish to deliver him a stinging setdown.

He inclined his head in the faintest approximation of a bow. "Good night."

Meg fumed as she and Livy followed Mrs. Leland up the stairs and through dim and twisting corridors. At last the woman opened the door of a large room with a newly lit fire and three glowing lamps. The footman set down their bags.

"Your supper will be here soon," the housekeeper said, then shut the door behind her, leaving Meg and Livy alone.

Meg threw herself upon the bed, pounding her fists into the silken counterpane. "Livy, that man is the most disagreeable person I have ever had the misfortune to encounter."

"Meggy, we cannot blame him for our own misunderstandings. These are very fine accommodations."

"He is laughing at us. I know he finds us pathetic and insignificant, a pair of country dowds."

"Yes, I suppose he does."

"I cannot bear being thought a swindler, even by the likes of him."

The next morning Meg awoke when two maids entered, one with a breakfast tray, the other with fresh hot water. After stirring the fire and opening the draperies to reveal bright sun through the sheer curtains, one spoke shyly. "A message from his lordship, miss. He will send for you later this morning." After brief curtsies, the maids went out.

Meg rolled out of bed and sank her toes into the deep plush of the carpet. The tray was crowded with an array of dishes and a steaming pot of chocolate. She poured two cups, handed one to Livy, and walked over to the window, pushing the silk curtain aside.

A smooth lawn stretched off toward a copse of trees and a distant lake shimmering in the sunlight. Several sleek horses grazed on a near rise, while the distant hills bore the fluffy dots of far-off sheep. The scene was so idyllic, Meg's fingers itched to find paper and pen before she took a second sip of chocolate. As Livy joined her at the window, Meg watched the earl canter off on the same gray that had carried him last night.

"I hope he is on his way back to London alone," Meg said to Livy. "But I suppose he is just out for a morning ride to impress his tenants and terrorize any sluggards among them."

Livy sighed. "Do you think such magnificent good looks and a wicked tongue always go hand in hand?"

"Probably has something to do with his heritage. Just pray that his grandmother will not be worse. We have no choice but to throw ourselves on the mercy of the countess."

Two

Having changed out of his riding clothes, Nicholas Barrington Wadsworth, the tenth earl of Wakefield, stared into the mirror. What the deuce had he been thinking? Tearing off to Berkshire last night with those two chits over some worthless trinket. His grandmother had dozens of old fans. He should have sent the Haywards on their way without regard to any fan, worthless or not. Why had he even bothered to talk to Miss Hayward in the first place?

Devil take it, he couldn't tie his wretched cravat for the life of him. He stripped it off, threw it on the chair, and grabbed another. Unbidden, he thought again of Miss Hayward's adorable face and earnest words. Was she simply a fetching little forger, or did her story hold water?

Carefully he tried to fold a section of the neckcloth, twisting the knot as he thought his valet did. Miss Hayward's stubborn refusal to hand over the real antique had caused this entire escapade. Why would she want a mere copy, an admittedly fraudulent work, in return for the valuable fan he had paid for? Damn and blast, the knot was backward in the mirror and the whole thing ridiculously upside down.

Miss Margaret Hayward had been the perfect cap to a perfect day. Perfectly dreadful, that is, beginning with a report on serious drainage problems on his Yorkshire estate, followed by his rogue of a nephew's arrival. As usual, Jason had reeked of gin, his fortification for the customary scene the two played like seasoned thespians. The final act always concluded with Nicholas extracting a promise from Jason to keep his gaming under control and Jason extracting from Nicholas a generous bank draft.

Nicholas should have followed his immediate reaction when Jason left and retreated to his club. Then he never would have met Meg, as her sister called her. She was a clever minx. No, that designation had the ring of harmless prank to it. Ingenious little swindler was more like it.

He tossed another crumpled cravat on the growing pile. Actually, she showed impressive courage, considering she dressed little better than a dairymaid. But she sounded like a lady, and her spirit, even in the face of his anger, showed determination.

Lord, he had been preposterous, just as pompous as those satin-clad dandies in White's bow window. A few pounds and she would have been on her way, no doubt. She was rather a good-looking lass. Perhaps her clear-eyed beauty as much as her fortitude charmed him. Her natural radiance made an enchanting contrast to the overdressed, overperfumed, and vacuous ladies of the *ton,* his usual company. He hated to admit he found her quite eye-catching, that something in her countenance had struck him like a bolt from the blue.

Why couldn't he manage this ordinarily mindless task? Discarding another neckcloth, Nick tried to sweep the vision of Miss Hayward from his mind. All he wanted was to get that worthless copied fan from his grandmother, give it to Miss Hayward for the real thing, then send those two chits back to town. This very morning.

He had no intention whatsoever of altering his carefully planned system of annual reviews of estate business. He had arrived one day early for his summer residence, but the rest of his household would come today, according to previous arrangements. Tomorrow he would begin meetings with his steward, reviewing the tenant records, evaluating improvement needs, and forecasting production. Next week the steward of his Yorkshire estates would arrive for more of the same. Then he would return with the man to Yorkshire to attend to the properties in person.

Nicholas cast aside two more creased ties. He was entirely faithful to his grandfather's yearly routines, for who could quarrel with the successes of many decades? Even though his father did his very best to drive the estates into the River Tick, only now, two years after his father's death and Nick's assumption of the title, were things returning to reasonable efficiency. He would let nothing stand in the way of continual betterment. So today he would deal with the fan silliness and be prepared for tomorrow without upset.

Enough nonsense for a lifetime, he fumed, trying the simplest bow. He tried to visualize Miss Hayward in one of the guest rooms. Would she be defiant, as she had been yesterday? Or would the long drive and the influence of the Hall have tempered her indignation?

The thought of her staring at the Apollo in his London house . . . What the deuce! The bow now sagged like a noose before the hangman got to work. Perhaps if he pleated a section of the neckcloth very carefully, the folds would look better.

Had it been fascination in her eyes? Or mere shock? It had been obvious she was staring directly at . . . damn, if this wasn't even worse! Another crumpled cravat joined the pile on the chair. How Eason, his valet, would snicker if he saw the heap of concessions to helplessness. Once more Nick put a stiffly pressed model around his neck.

He held one starched end of the tie in each hand, then crossed them with great care, peering into the mirror. The absurdity of his dilemma made him smile. Over and under. His expression of rapt attention to the knot appeared quite ludicrous, and he laughed out loud. What in the world was he doing? He, the tenth Earl of Wakefield, was unable to knot his cravat because he was mooning over a wench whose nonsensical purpose was disordering his own well-regulated life? Preposterous. He stifled his laughter and cleared his throat.

At a tap on the door he called, "Come in."

"The countess invites you to join her in the salon," Sutton said. "Here, let me assist you, milord."

Nicholas submitted to the butler's deft ministrations. In no time at all, Sutton arranged the cravat flawlessly.

"Thank you very much, Sutton."

"My pleasure, Lord Wakefield."

When Nicholas reached his grandmother, she presented her cheek for a kiss. "I assume there is a delicious story to be told. You do not often arrive in the middle of the night with two young ladies in tow. Did you bring them for my edification or for your own purposes?"

Before he could begin to explain, he followed her gaze to the footman opening the door for the Misses Hayward. Nick glanced away as soon as he saw them, but his eyes were drawn back as ardently as bees throng to a bloom of clover.

Miss Hayward's modest gown of sprigged muslin and her rustic knit shawl suggested a guileless country girl with no artifice. Her honey-blond hair was drawn into a topknot and tied with a single narrow ribbon. The very simplicity of her appearance was precisely calculated to strengthen her claim of innocence. A very clever miss, indeed. But those wide blue eyes, so candid, so sincere, those velvety pink lips, so trembling, so naive, those tiny white hands, so open, so vulnerable . . .

He turned abruptly and inspected the folds of the window draperies. "You may tell your story to the countess," he said without looking back at the young ladies.

"My lady, I am Margaret Hayward, and this is my sister, Olivia. We come from Cawthorn Manor in Sussex. I fear we have all been victims of a dreadful misunderstanding."

Nick tried to keep looking away from her, but he could not. With his countenance as stern as possible, he turned and feasted his eyes upon the sight of her. She was the unlikeliest-looking temptress he had ever beheld.

"Hayward," the countess mused. "That sounds familiar. Perhaps it will come to me later."

"I believe you have a story to tell the countess," he urged.

"Our friend Gaston LeClerque lost his family and his livelihood in France," Meg said, her voice quivering but her demeanor brave as a warrior queen. "As a refugee, he has no income. But he has a little shop. He sells things he brought from France or sometimes things other refugees want to sell. And sometimes, things my family makes."

She sounded very convincing, Nick thought. Quite the adept actress?

"One of his prized possessions is an antique fan that belonged to Madame de Pompadour. He asked me to copy the design and make similar fans he could sell. Gaston gave me the silk. It was old, but I thought he had no means to secure new. I took the design from the antique fan, as he wished, and made three copies. I knew he planned to sell them. When I learned Gaston sold one of my copies to Lord Wakefield as the original, I knew I had to—" She paused, her eyes sparkling with unshed tears.

The countess raised her eyebrows, pursed her lips, and looked at Nicholas, then back at Meg. "Go on."

"I destroyed the other replicas. I must have the third copy back. I asked Lord Wakefield, but he had given it to you as a gift, my lady."

"Nicholas, send a footman for that fan, if you please."

The footman dispatched, Nicholas stepped close to his grandmother and spoke softly in her ear. "You cannot possibly believe such rubbish, Grandmama."

"Why, Nicky," she whispered. "I do believe you suffer from injured pride. Apparently you are embarrassed to have been duped."

Perhaps, he thought, Grandmama was right. "I was deliberately misled. But did you question the fan's authenticity? All these years, I believed you were the antique expert!"

"Touché, Lord Wakefield," the countess murmured.

Nick resumed his position beside the window. He could see from the twinkle in her eyes that Grandmama was treating this whole incident as rather a lark. And he certainly found the whole situation ludicrous. But Miss Hayward was tenacious in proclaiming her innocence.

After only a few moments, the countess took the fan brought to her by the footman and examined it carefully. She opened it and peered at the design, then up at Meg. "My dear, you said you painted this fan yourself?"

"Yes, my lady, I did."

"Come close, Nicholas, and inspect her handiwork."

On the silk leaf, a lute-playing cavalier serenaded a shepherdess in the arcadian serenity of a pastoral scene. A grove of spring trees, verdant flowered branches, and clusters of pastel blossoms formed a charming setting for the loving couple. To the earl's eye, every intricate brushstroke evidenced the skill of the artist.

"La, I would say you have a rare gift, Miss Hayward," the countess said.

"Lady Wakefield, I have the real fan for you." Meg handed the pouch to the countess, who removed the old fan, spreading it wide and comparing the two.

"Look here, Nicholas. You can hardly tell the difference. This is good enough to deceive any expert I can think of."

He used his quizzing glass to magnify the designs. "Yes, almost a perfect duplicate. Except . . ."

He faced Meg squarely. "If you painted this so recently, Miss Hayward, and your sister mounted the silk on the sticks, why are there signs of soil and wear on the one you claim is a copy?"

Meg said nothing.

"This, in my opinion, is clear evidence of attempted fraud. You contrived to make the new fan look old. Banged it up, rubbed a bit of ash on it. Definitely the work of a swindler." Her face grew whiter, and she clasped her shaking hands, but her head remained high.

Nicholas winked at his grandmama. "If you do not wish to call the constable, I shall send the pair of them back to London this afternoon."

"May I have my copy?" Meg asked.

"Of course," Nick said, not knowing which one to hand her.

When he hesitated, Meg grabbed one of the fans and with deft twists, tore it to pieces.

"What the—" Nick exclaimed.

"Oh, my dear," the countess cried. "Your own handiwork . . ."

"Now there is only one Fontainebleau fan, the original," Meg declared. Miss Olivia put her arm around her sister's waist and stood close.

Nicholas couldn't take his eyes from the mangled remains of the fan in Meg's hands. He hadn't meant to goad her to this.

"Now, my lady, if we could return to town? Our family will be worried," Meg said.

"A few more moments won't hurt." Lady Wakefield carefully folded her antique fan. "Nicholas, please ring for tea. Sit down, gels."

Nick gazed at Meg, who caught her lower lip in her teeth and stared at the floor.

"Miss Hayward," he began. "I feel I must—"

She cast him a look of such outright distaste, he stopped in surprise.

Abruptly the countess banged her jewel-encrusted

stick on the floor. "Nicholas, while we are waiting, would you please show the Misses Hayward my new conservatory?"

"As you wish, Grandmama," Nicholas answered. What was she up to? Why she wanted these chits to see the new conservatory was beyond his ken.

In truth, he was very pleased with her delight in the new room, for it had been his suggestion. Her achy joints almost completely deprived her of enjoyment of her gardens. Now the blooms would be indoors, where she could savor her flowers in warmth and comfort every day.

And indeed, as he stepped into the sun-drenched room with semicircular walls and ceiling made of glass, he felt as if the outdoors had come inside. Two workmen plastered the sections of wall, formerly the exterior of the house, on either side of the door from the salon. Only five flat pilasters supported the metal web holding roof panes of glass.

The young ladies stared about them in wonder.

"It is quite the latest thing," he said. "When finished, we will fill the room with plants, perhaps some lemon trees from the orangery, and even some exotic species from the south seas."

Miss Meg Hayward walked over to the glass and gazed out. The sunlight crowned her hair with shining gold, creating an aura around her that seemed to light her from within. Nicholas could hardly stop himself from trying to capture her glow in his hands. What the devil was bothering him anyway? He stared at the beds of budding tulips beyond the glass until the young ladies started back to the countess.

Back in the salon, Lady Wakefield was waiting with an expression that to Nicholas promised an outrageous scheme. "What did you think of my conservatory?" she asked.

"Very lovely, your ladyship," Meg said, her voice hardly more than a whisper.

"I think it requires a bit of embellishment, perhaps some . . ." Lady Wakefield paused as the butler and footman arrived with a huge silver tray bearing pots, cups, and a plate of iced cakes.

Nick took his unwanted tea without comment. The faster they finished, the sooner he could send the young ladies on their way. The farce had gone too far already.

He tried to read the expression on Meg's face, but without success. Her eyes were luminous, her lips unsmiling. Judging strictly on appearance, he would never doubt her innocence.

"So, my dear." The countess addressed Miss Hayward. "What can you do about it?"

Nick was startled by the question. Meg looked equally confused.

"I am at your ladyship's mercy," Meg said.

"What mercy is that?" the countess asked. "Can you do it?"

"I do not understand, my lady."

"Paint. Decorate. Adorn my conservatory walls with flowers and designs."

Nicholas felt his jaw drop open.

Meg slumped back against her chair. "Paint flowers on the walls?" she asked in a hoarse voice.

"Exactly. Nicholas has brought you to me exactly at the moment I need you."

"But . . ." Meg began.

Good God, Nicholas thought. What was Grandmama up to? This farce wasn't over after all.

"I will gladly hire you the finest painters in the realm, Grandmama. As soon as I return to London, I shall begin the search."

"That will not be necessary. I have settled on Miss Hayward. I intend to provide a generous stipend for the young ladies, and I am looking forward to their company for the next few weeks. What word do we need to send to your people, Miss Hayward?"

Nicholas watched Miss Hayward reach for her sister's hand and squeeze it.

"I believe we can compose a letter to Father this afternoon," she said.

"Then it is decided," Lady Wakefield said. "I am quite fond of roses. Masses of roses of all shades. Nicholas, please take Miss Hayward into the library and find her some paper and writing implements for her letters and to make a list of materials we need for the project."

"Of course, Grandmama," he said. "Miss Hayward?"

After he closed the door behind them, Nicholas bowed to Meg. "Congratulations. I presume you have accomplished your purpose, though I am not clear exactly what your aim could be."

"You are too kind, Lord Wakefield."

The acid tone of insincerity in her voice was no more than he deserved, Nick thought. "Go with Sutton now. He will take care of your needs."

Her eyebrows arched at a rather insolent slant, she followed the butler. Nick watched her for a moment before heading in the opposite direction.

His neat and systematic world tipped precariously. Miss Meg Hayward and her sister at Wakefield Hall for several weeks? Not a tranquil thought. He could not allow any interference in his examination of the estates. Postponing his meetings was unthinkable.

Yet, he had a strong notion to send his household servants back to London as soon as they arrived to-night and follow himself tomorrow. What a nuisance, but he had no wish to stay here at the Hall with the young ladies in residence. Why, he was not precisely certain.

"You wished to speak with me, Grandmama," Nicholas said, entering her afternoon sitting room.

The countess took off her spectacles and placed them in her work bag. "You are planning to stay here for a month or two, Nicky?"

"Perhaps not. I, ah, must be back in town soon. I have obligations. . . ." Nicholas reached for a specific occasion but came up blank.

"Of course you do. I know there are important gatherings every evening. Activities of crucial import." She waved him to a chair.

"You are teasing me."

"No, I am entirely serious. I wish to know if you have made any progress toward finding yourself a countess?"

Nicholas stretched his legs out before him and grimaced. "A particularly insipid collection of misses this year."

"Ah, me. I find you rather tragic, Nicky. A victim of one fickle gel so long ago. Now you pine away as though you worshipped her from afar."

"Poppycock! I've never heard anything so absurd. I've told you a thousand times, Cynthia meant nothing to me."

"Your sisters and I disagree. You must be suffering from a broken heart."

"Fustian."

"Seven years now, Nicholas . . . if you are not lost to love, certainly there would have been someone."

There had been quite a few someones over the years, Nicholas thought, but not the kind of someones his grandmama should hear about. "I am quite confident no one in London remembers I once cared for Cynthia."

"Are you certain? Others must wonder why you have formed no attachments."

"Mincing, lisping females without a particle of brain matter do not interest me a whit."

"You are missing so much, especially parenthood."

Good lord, usually he was able to keep her from tricking him into these conversations. "Believe me, Grandmama, I intend to marry someday. I am sympathetic with your hope to see a great-grandson and heir."

"I shall not live forever."

"But I suspect you shall try. And I suspect you shall see an heir apparent before too much time passes."

The countess sniffed in derision. "I would guess London is rather thin of company at this time of year."

Nicholas changed the subject. "Are you certain you want Miss Hayward to paint in your conservatory?"

"Her work is exquisite."

"I wish to point out, Grandmama, that we know her ability only as a copyist. And on a very small scale."

"Nicholas, I am so pleased that you always consider my best interests. You are indeed a loving grandson and a worthy successor to your grandfather."

Nicholas bowed to her, not deceived for a moment

by her deliberate misinterpretation. "Thank you. I am proud to receive your approbation. Now, as to Miss Hayward."

"I think I remember her family. Some years ago her father read papers at the Royal Society. The Old Earl was most interested in his theories."

"How interesting."

"I do not remember what he was doing, but perhaps it shall come to me. I seem to recall he holds a barony."

"Many excellent painters have considerable experience adorning the chambers of our finest houses. No doubt we could find someone of distinguished stature to execute the latest in design."

"Nicky, you are ever so considerate. But I assure you the young ladies and I shall get along famously. I have every confidence in Miss Hayward's talent. She is a most clever puss."

Nicholas tussled with an urge to laugh out loud. "The scale of her work in the conservatory will be many times greater than her work on the fan."

"And will it not be a wonder to behold?"

Nicholas shrugged. "I sincerely hope so. But this is your whim, Grandmama. I shall say nothing further. You and Miss Hayward may decorate the conservatory in any fashion you desire, even in one of Prinny's outrageous Oriental modes."

"Why, Nicky, what a lovely idea. Perhaps with tigers and elephants prominently featured."

"Quite." He rose to go, thoroughly amused by the exchange.

"Gracious, I have quite forgotten to mention why I called you here."

"Not to discuss my marital status? Or your plans for the conservatory?"

"Your birthday, Nicholas."

He winced a bit at the thought. "Next month."

"Yes, of course. I want to have a festive celebration for all the tenants and the village. And a grand ball for all our friends. You must have the best observance ever for your thirtieth birthday."

The earl's smile faded. No sense wasting his energy protesting. Opposition to the party would be completely ineffective. In some matters, Grandmama would always have her way.

Nicholas strode toward the stables, filling his lungs with the brisk spring air and fighting back the urge to smash his fist into something solid. The last thing he needed was any diversion from his carefully drawn plans, particularly the distraction offered by the proximity of a petite artist with a mass of tawny curls, a lush mouth, and tempting curves. And now a birthday ball to worry about, no doubt to be filled with hen-witted young ladies and their mamas, all on campaigns to leg-shackle him.

His plans were set, and he did not intend to turn back. He would devote every ounce of his energy for the next five years to restoring the Wakefield estates to the prosperity his grandfather had built. How his father could have wastreled away his life and fortune was simply incomprehensible.

Nicholas slowed his pace to watch the tilers on the stable roof. If the wind damage had been repaired ten years ago as it should have been, he wouldn't have had to repair the rotten timbers and replace every last tile. Between the roof and the construction of the conservatory, almost every penny from the sale of his father's string of racing horses was gone already. Every single tenant's cottage needed attention. And he intended to open negotiations with Squire Grennan about buying some of the neighboring acreage.

The way he planned the next five years, by the time he turned thirty-five, the estates would be running as smoothly and making as much profit as in his grandfather's day. The Old Earl, as everyone thought of him, had dedicated himself to the well-being of every person on his land. Even though he had grown up with no expectations whatsoever, Nick was determined to reject the loose ways of his father. His model was his grandfather, and in caring for the Wakefield estates, he dedicated himself to emulate the Old Earl's example.

And an entirely unwelcome pair of saucy pink lips had nothing to do with his purposes. Perhaps he ought to return to London and stay away from those lips.

He picked up his pace again, skirting the stacks of tiles in the stable yard. In London, he wouldn't have to see Miss Hayward every day. She had an intriguing sort of appeal, a combination of naiveté and determined spirit, unlike the flirtatious and often suggestive polish of the *haut ton*'s females. Come to think of it, Meg was the first young lady who engaged his fancy in a very long time. How very strange!

Nick leaned on the paddock fence and admired the three burly mares and their sturdy foals. How Father would have laughed if he had seen his bloodstock replaced with these hearty draught animals. Instead of fleet-footed vitality, the horses here today were full of muscle and stamina, the strength to pull wagons instead of running in circles to entertain fellows who should have better things to do.

But Nicholas felt he should not leave Wakefield Hall just then. After his morning meeting with his attorney the previous day, he had no more concerns in town for the rest of the month other than a stack of social invitations. What if the girl's only ability was as a copyist? What if her skill on a small surface such as the fan did not translate to an entire wall? He needed to keep an eye on things. He could get busy on the repairs to tenants' cottages. If he stayed away from the main house, he would have minimal contact with Meg, and he could keep the situation under control.

The larger of the two mares ambled over and Nicholas scratched her ears. And what was the problem anyway? So Meg was a pretty young chit, and hardly the first to have caught his eye. No woman had ever breached his defenses yet, though some had tried. He could not imagine what was wrong with him now, worrying about this little nobody.

He could clearly remember her every nuance. "You are too kind, Lord Wakefield," she had said in a tone that clearly meant she thought he was a consummate knave. If she was used to dealing with people like that LeClerque fellow, no wonder she had a bad impression of human nature. Plus, Nick had to admit, his temper had been quite keen. An afternoon listening to more of Jason's contretemps had him in a tearing rage already. Then to find he was the victim of a swindle, just like the greenest recruit buying certified solid gold reliquaries before he left the docks in Portugal!

He reached down and pulled a handful of the fresh young grass just out of the mare's reach on his side of the fence. Her ears pricked forward and she snuffled in anticipation. No, he would not flee to London. He would stay here and look out for Grandmama, make sure she got her money's worth in painting. It would take only a day or two to cure himself of the girl's absurd allure. Her blue eyes and honey hair were really quite ordinary, found in every hamlet in the realm. He could keep his bearing thoroughly correct: cool, proper, and dignified. Nothing to it.

Nicholas fed the mare another handful of grass and smoothed her forelock. Miss Hayward, however delectable, was not going to turn him from his essential determination to devote his energy to these estates.

Nicholas despised men who could not keep their emotions under control. Poets who mooned on and on about love were weak and pathetic. Someday, of course, he intended to find himself an ideal countess and ensure the succession. But so-called *love* would have nothing to do with it.

Three

Livy sat on a blue satin boudoir chair, smoothing the skirt of her sprigged muslin day dress. "Do you think the countess will let us stay in this elegant room, or will we have to move to the servants' quarters?" she asked.

"I suppose she will." Meg stroked the brush through Livy's soft nut-brown hair.

"Suppose what, to stay or move?"

"As to that . . ." Meg's voice drifted off. She continued her rhythmic strokes, slowly drawing the brush from the crown of Livy's head to the very end of each wavy strand.

"Meg, I don't think you are attending me."

"You said you wanted to move to the attic?"

"Of course I do. I want to spin dust into cobwebs and play with the spiders."

"I am sure the countess will allow you to do whatever you wish."

"Perhaps I can even find a few bats under the eaves."

"How very lovely, dear." Meg put down the brush and wandered to the window, where she pushed aside the sheer curtain.

The oldest wing of the house swept off to the left, topped by a battlemented tower on which a bright flag snapped in the breeze. To the right, a classical portico graced the red brick addition. Clearly the generations of Wakefield earls simply added whatever they desired to the previous generations' tastes. The building was sprawling and very, very grand, its total effect boasting of the family's ancient and important history.

Livy limped to Meg's side. "What are you thinking about? You must be a hundred miles away."

"Mmmm."

"Meggy, did his lordship apologize to you?"

"Of course not. He congratulated me in a most sarcastic tone. I wish I had some clever riposte ready for him, but I did not. Just my very best frown."

"Oh, my, Meg, you are very naughty! When Lord Wakefield spoke to me, I tried to be accommodating."

"Accommodating? Pooh! Next time I see him, I just may give him a proper set-down."

Livy flinched. "You would not!"

Meg turned away from the window and caught a glimpse of her reflection in the mirror. "How I wish I had a decent gown." She wrinkled her nose at her simple pale green muslin.

"We are a strange-looking pair of inhabitants for this elegant room," Livy observed. "If I didn't know better, I would think this was Windsor Castle."

Meg nodded. She yearned to give herself a touch of elegance. In the presence of the toplofty Lord High-and-Haughty she wanted to be cool, proper, and dignified, admirable in looks as well as words. She would simply have to rise above her lack of fashionable attire and think up a barbed remark. Yes, a stab of wit, a spike of cutting repartee accompanied by the slash of her disdainful smirk, and he would receive his just reward for treating them with such high-handed pomposity.

"Your turn," Livy said, brandishing the brush.

Meg sat down and closed her eyes. Each stroke through her hair helped to calm her thoughts. "I simply do not know what to tell the countess."

"Tell her? Tell her about what?"

"Tell her whether or not I can decorate her conservatory."

Livy gasped. "Meg, do not say you are considering a refusal? Turn down two hundred pounds?"

"I have never painted on a wall, Livy. The largest thing I ever painted was a piece of paper eighteen inches square."

"Oh, dear, I hadn't thought of that. But most of the walls are of glass."

"The two plaster walls on either side of the doors from the drawing room are at least fifteen feet tall and half again as wide. To me, the area looks as vast as the facade of Westminster Abbey."

"But, Meggy, two hundred pounds . . ."

"Exactly. Two hundred pounds is more money than we have ever seen. We will be well on our way to outfitting Dorie and Bea for a London Season and the capture of two wealthy gentlemen."

"Or we could make repairs to the house and buy a few sheep for the meadow."

"Or we could hire one of those balloons and spend every cent drifting above the countryside! You know our best hope is to marry off one of the girls. Please, Livy, do not start thinking up new plans for our future."

"I am sorry, but I cannot stop worrying about what

kind of husbands they will find if all they look for is a fortune."

Meg shrugged. "I also worry about their choices. That is why we must have enough money to turn them out in style. Aunt Sylvia moves in the right circles, and by next year all her daughters will be safely wed. If Dorie and Bea make a good impression on her, Aunt Sylvia is sure to agree to sponsor them."

"And in the meantime, we continue stitching sachets and selling eggs and practicing on a harpsichord that hasn't been tuned for ages." Livy wore a completely crestfallen look.

Meg hugged her sister. "You are actually saying, 'Look at all this splendor. This is what I was born to have,' are you not?"

"If Mama had not died, Father would have kept up his interest in the estate. We would not be so poor, and he would not hide in his laboratory all day, and . . ." Now it was Livy's turn to let her voice fade away.

Meg sighed and shook her head. "I will have to tell the countess I have never painted a wall. Even if she still wants me, I could end up working for weeks and not satisfying her. Or myself, not to mention that supercilious grandson, Lord High-and-Haughty himself. Then what?"

"Meg, I know you can paint wonderful scenes. Can you not enlarge some sketches, one to cover each wall? Most of the high work will be clouds and sky. You should not utter one word of doubt to Lady Wakefield or the earl either. Not until you have tried."

"And if I decide to swim across the Channel, I guess you think I should not ask for help until I am halfway to France." Meg laughed in spite of herself.

"Give yourself credit for a bit of courage. I have

never known you to avoid a task because it involved developing a new skill."

"Now you are saying that you will never forgive me if I do not try," Meg said, raising her eyebrows in challenge.

"As a matter of fact, I think I am saying just that."

"In all honesty, I cannot argue with your view. I probably would never forgive myself if I did not try to earn this two hundred pounds. Only promise you will give me encouragement if I falter, sister dear."

Livy wrapped her arms around Meg and held her tight. "I promise."

"Then I shall try my very best. And now are you ready to go down for dinner?"

Meg and Livy paused just inside the Ivory Salon. The footman who showed them in bowed politely and backed out of the room, closing the door behind them.

"Don't gawk, Livy."

"I cannot help myself. Do you think the king's throne room is this magnificent?"

Meg could hardly believe her eyes. She forgot her intention to remain coolly disdainful and ready to give the earl a bit of a set-down. She slowly walked toward a huge painting between the windows. "This must be a Boucher."

"What is a boo-shay?"

"François Boucher, a French painter, whose works are among the finest in the world." She stared at the canvas, drinking in every detail of the sweeping bucolic scene of handsome peasants and their animals on a rocky hillside.

"Do you think the portrait above the fireplace is Lady Wakefield?"

Meg tore her stare from the peasants to find the striking full-length rendition of an elegant lady in a broad-brimmed multiplumed hat. The dainty figure linked her hand through the arm of a refined gentleman in powdered wig and knee breeches, and with her other hand she petted a fluffy white dog.

"I recognize the countess. I suspect the painter was Sir Thomas Gainsborough."

"Correct on both counts, Miss Hayward." The earl joined them in the center of the room. "The gentleman is my grandfather, the eighth earl."

"You have a most disconcerting tendency to materialize from thin air, my lord," Meg said.

"And you have an incurable propensity to concentrate on works of art. Would you care for a glass of sherry? Miss Olivia?"

Meg declined for them both, trying to shed the sensation of being rather out of place. Even the dainty porcelain baubles in the room illustrated the nobility of this house and its family. And just as absolutely, made lesser mortals feel insignificant. How could she paint scenes to satisfy the countess?

Meg watched Lord Wakefield go to the sideboard and fill three crystal glasses with a golden liquid. The earl already had a poor opinion of her. To earn her two hundred pounds, she would be competing with the finest artists in England and France.

Lord Wakefield offered her the tray and she took a glass. If he had stepped out of another portrait by one of the world's greatest artists, his appearance could not have been a more perfect example of well-tailored elegance. His dark brown hair was slicked straight back from his forehead, his whole face shining with the sunny look of the outdoors. His waistcoat was creamy beige, just two or three shades lighter than his sleek inexpressibles that hugged his long legs until disappearing into the burnished leather of his Hessian boots. The soft gray-green of his coat cast a rustic effect over the whole ensemble, indeed the epitome of country aristocracy.

"Grandmama will join us directly." He gave a sherry to Livy and raised his own in the air. "To an enjoyable stay for you at Wakefield Hall."

"Thank you, Lord Wakefield," Livy said.

"Yes, thank you." Meg took a swallow, then recoiled in surprise as she tasted tart liquid. "If you please, Lord Wakefield, I would rather have—"

She stopped at the sight of his smile, dazzling, though tinged with mockery, she suspected.

"Yes?" he asked.

"Meg," Livy whispered. "I have never . . ."

"Thank you for the sherry." Meg threw Livy a warning wink.

"You are quite welcome." Lord Wakefield hurried to his grandmama's side as she entered, supported by Sutton. They placed pillows behind her, and she sat down, heavily for one so otherwise delicate. To Meg, the countess seemed to be moving with considerable pain.

"Here, gels." Lady Wakefield patted the satin cushions on either side of her.

"Your portrait is very lovely, my lady." Meg sat but directed her gaze above the fireplace.

"Oh, yes, one of Gainsborough's most popular talents was his ability to make his every subject look like an angel. I believe he added at least five feathers to my hat and subtracted several inches from, well, let me simply say he was adept at the most cunning flattery."

"Grandmama, no one believes that for an instant." Nicholas addressed Meg and Livy. "The countess is widely reputed to be the most beautiful woman in Berkshire. It is said that every man in London begged to court her, beginning when she was barely fifteen."

"Pay no attention to Nicholas, gels, he can be a sad rascal with his ostentatious compliments."

"Which you adore!" Nicholas brought her a glass of sherry on the silver tray.

"No matter how many suitors you had, my lady, I think you chose a very fine-looking husband," Livy said, gesturing to the portrait.

"Indeed I did. The Old Earl was a man who took great pleasure in serving his king, his family, and his tenants. Everyone admired him."

Meg thought she could see the bright glimmer of a tear, but the countess sipped her sherry and changed the subject.

"Are you comfortable in your rooms?"

"Oh, yes. Meg and I simply fear our traveling things are hardly up to the grandeur of our surroundings," Livy said.

The countess patted her knee. "Of course, my dear. That is why we have decided not to dress for dinner. Why stand on ceremony? We shall simply enjoy each other's company."

Meg stole a glance at Lord Wakefield. In his formal dress clothes he would be even more formidable. And even more irresistible.

"Would you care for more sherry?" he asked, taking her empty glass.

"Please." Where had her drink disappeared?

Meg rose and walked to his side as he poured more sherry into her glass. She wanted to show him she was not completely awed by him. She spoke in a soft tone, to him alone.

"I am very gratified to see that you indeed are able to smile, my lord."

"What? Of course I can smile."

"Yesterday in London I never would have believed it. I was afraid you were sorely afflicted with the sourest of dispositions."

He gazed at her steadily, and she felt a twinge of regret for the impertinence of her words. Not that he didn't deserve all the censure she could summon. It was just that she was suddenly tongue-tied, mesmerized by his deep-set dark eyes. She was close enough to count every one of his long black lashes. Grabbing one hand with her other, she barely resisted reaching up to trace his smile lines and touch his newly shaven jaw to feel if it was as smooth as it looked.

"I suppose," he said in a soft undertone, "you expected to be tossed into my moldy old dungeon."

The moment shattered. "More likely abandoned in the woods for your pack of wild boars to devour."

"Oh, my menagerie is well fed. But I have not had a soul in the dungeon for months."

"How utterly shocking! One would have assumed at least a band of gypsies would be in residence."

Nicholas lowered his voice to a whisper. "If I were to toss you anywhere, Miss Hayward, I would choose far better environs."

Face burning, Meg drained her glass. Again, he left her speechless.

"Dinner is served, my lady," Sutton announced.

* * *

Nicholas regretted his remark the moment it passed his lips. Far too suggestive and entirely out of line, he concluded as he helped the countess to the table.

Fortunately Miss Hayward seemed temporarily captivated by another roomful of old masters and family portraits. At dinner, Nicholas paid scant attention to the conversation and hardly tasted his food. The radiance of the candlelight complimented Miss Meg Hayward's rosy complexion, and her golden hair gleamed like sunbeams through pure, clear honey. He wished the sherry had paralyzed his tongue.

First he had accused the young lady of being a scoundrel and a swindler, then he turned right around to insult her with a most suggestive comment totally unworthy of both of them. Unthinkable that he could have made such a coarse statement, but the words had simply tumbled out and couldn't be coaxed back.

Miss Hayward did not cast her eyes in his direction. Good Lord, what to do now? He must seem the most boorish man she ever encountered. And his strange, almost perverse fascination with her?

Nicholas stabbed a morsel of beef and chewed, though the meat seemed flat and flavorless. Nothing in his experience explained Miss Hayward's singular allure. She really had no more than ordinary looks, pretty but quite unpolished. Perhaps it was her gumption, her willingness to face off with him, no matter how she might dread the consequences. Hardly the missish, clinging demeanor one expected in a chit of her age.

He stole a look at her, engaged in animated conversation with his grandmama. Maybe the fact she thought him an ogre was a good thing. If she took him in strong dislike, the next few weeks might be easier. He would spend his time examining every facet of the estate, perhaps attend a few market days and horse fairs to search for more strong-boned mares. He would simply ignore the progress of the conservatory painting. If the countess did not receive her money's worth, she had no one to blame but herself. And he would hardly have to see Miss Hayward at all.

Meg let herself into the dark conservatory. A quick glance around confirmed her solitude, and she collapsed into a chair, letting her tension drain away. During dinner she had sealed a sweet smile upon her face and tempered her remarks to gentle platitudes while her anger simmered.

Knave, churl, fop . . . how dared he speak of . . . of whatever he meant by his lewd remark. Toss indeed!

Or perhaps he meant to toss her from a high battlement or off a sheer cliff. No! The glitter in his eyes spoke of couches or beds and showed her exactly what kind of wench he thought she was. She, Meg Hayward, daughter of a man who once read papers at the Royal Society, a man of science who had a distinguished reputation. Or once had, since he no longer made any effort to publish his work.

She bounced to her feet and began to pace. All the earl saw was a female who painted fans to keep her family from hunger. Lord Wakefield's attitude was unconscionable, however common among some titled families. The more Meg thought about Lord Wakefield, the faster and harder she stomped.

Boys like Nicholas Wadsworth were brought up to

disdain all but their equals or betters, to view life with snobbish superiority. He never wanted for a thing, she supposed, never had anything but bowing and scraping from menials, never had to do anything to earn society's regard. All he truly had was a name. A few pitiful words put him beyond reproach, however undeserving he was in truth. One more remark like that tossing matter and she would simply go home. Let them find another painter.

Of course, he was kind and loving to his grandmother. She said he built the conservatory for her, which was a thoughtful thing to do for an elderly invalid who loves gardening. Not that family attachment excused his poor manners. The aristocracy was always far too wrapped up in their ancestors.

She looked around the dim conservatory. The countess wanted roses. Meg could cover the spaces in little time, then take her fee. While she painted, she would devise a fitting farewell speech to his high-and-haughtiness. He was utterly undeserving of his rank. He was insufferably self-important. He was obnoxiously rude. And so she would tell him.

But not yet! Not until she had her money and was ready to go home.

The thought of home nearly stilled her heart. Everything at Cawthorn Manor needed repair. Father thought of nothing but his experiments, as the house slowly crumbled around them.

Meg stopped at the glass walls and gazed out at the moonlit lawns. The half-moon, bright enough to dull the view of stars, poured its gleaming silver tones over the hills. From her bedroom window at home, she could watch the moon slice a shimmering path across the water of the Channel on a clear night.

With each passing day, poor Aunt Regina slipped ever farther into her distant world, and Aunt Alice could do no more than tend the chickens and bake the lemon tarts they sold every Friday.

All Meg's hopes for the future centered on her youngest sisters, Pandora and Beatrice, growing more beautiful with every month. One or both might make an excellent match, a marriage that could rescue them all. In the meantime, the sale of the tarts, the eggs, their sachets, her painted trinkets, kept them almost in comfort. Almost, if one ignored the roof leaks, the tumbledown dairy, the decaying stable that sheltered their dear donkey. There was always tea ready to brew for the vicar's visits and sweets to give at Christmas and on saints' days, but Meg resented every penny for such things. Her little stash of coins grew ever so slowly.

Blast that Gaston! She had spent many hours last winter on those fans, and the rascal had not once let on he planned to pass them off as actual antiques. As copies, she had hoped to net a few shillings for her secret fund. Instead, she had left the scraps of torn silk and shattered sticks on the elegant carpet of the salon.

Which brought her back to Wakefield Hall and how quickly she could spread paint across these walls.

She walked over to draw her fingers across the smooth plaster. Would paint adhere to this surface? Probably not for long. She wondered if the countess planned to have canvas applied first, by far the most reasonable scheme.

Meg turned away to see her dim reflection in the wall of glass. The canvas would be a complication. Perhaps a hindrance to swift completion.

"Excuse me, Miss Hayward," Lord Wakefield said.

"What?" Her heart jumped into her throat and pounded hard enough to steal her breath. Again, she hadn't sensed his presence until his voice startled her.

"I am sorry to disturb, but I have been looking for you. Would you like me to bring a lamp or some candles in here?"

Whatever was he up to now? More lewd remarks? And they were alone.

"No," she sputtered. "That's not . . . yes, yes, I think we need some light."

He started toward the hall.

"No, wait. We can simply join the others."

"In a moment. I find I must apply for your pardon, Miss Hayward."

"Granted. Now we can go—"

"Please. I assure you, I do not ordinarily blurt out such ill-considered comments."

She met his earnest gaze. "Apparently, you only think them."

The corner of his mouth twitched. "I shall endeavor to curb both my opinions and my tongue in the future."

"Do not overburden yourself, my lord." She walked briskly out of the conservatory, then turned and smiled. "The term 'gentleman' is elastic enough to fit almost anyone."

Meg could just about feel the force of his astonishment as she turned to hurry back to the Ivory Salon.

"Wait, Miss Hayward," he called.

She pretended not to hear and continued, slipping gratefully into a chair beside Livy and trying to conceal her ragged breathing.

". . . the people lined the roads and there were so many carriages in the drive, the party could hardly make their way to us."

"Lady Wakefield is telling me about the visit of the king and queen here," Livy explained.

"More than forty years ago," the countess said. "But I shall never forget a moment."

"I am sure you will not," Meg agreed.

"Where have you been hiding?" the countess asked.

"Not hiding, my lady. I was looking at the walls. I am inclined to think they ought to be covered with canvas. Otherwise I fear the paint will peel."

"Good thinking, Miss Hayward. I am sure you are correct."

Meg was startled to see the earl enter the room from the opposite side.

He agreed quickly and promised to speak to the plasterer first thing in the morning.

"Then," the countess continued, "when you have finished with him, I want you to drive Miss Hayward to the village for her supplies."

Meg watched Lord Wakefield's reactions flicker across his face. He frowned and opened his mouth as if to object, then sighed and shrugged. "Whatever you say, Grandmama."

He looked every bit as frustrated as Meg felt.

Four

"Look, Livy, the rain is pouring down on us, but we aren't the slightest bit wet." Meg twirled around the conservatory, listening to the water splashing on the glass roof. She actually ducked when she looked upward to see the rain aiming right at her face.

"We should be dripping wet. It appears we are outside, but, of course, we are not."

With a delighted smile, Livy shook her head in wonder. "The pattering of the rain on the glass creates a little melody. Listen, it is truly beautiful."

Meg drew in a deep breath, listening and savoring the freshness of spring rain, the clean scent of awakening buds, with the hint of damp mossy earth.

The rain promised her a lucky reprieve. Surely Lord Wakefield would postpone their visit to town if mud bogged the roads. Perhaps she could avoid his company for the entire day. She stood quietly for a few moments, watching the shower, then forced herself back to the task at hand.

"If you will write down the numbers, I will measure the walls." She handed a small notebook to Livy. "I can take advantage of the delay while the canvas is hung to make scale drawings of each design."

Meg climbed up the ladder Mr. Ames had left and slid the measuring stick as high on the wall as she could reach. Livy marked the lower end and Meg squinted above the stick. "I estimate another five feet up there, plus this five." She stepped down and measured from the mark to the floor. "Approximately fifteen feet in height."

"With your drawings, you can be assured the countess will approve of her decorations?"

"Exactly." But the trick would be to transform small pictures into wall-size panoramas. Meg stretched the stick across the width of the blank wall to the right of the doorway into the house, marked the end, and moved the stick from the mark to the edge of the glass wall.

"Say, nine and a half feet wide." Her usual working surface was about eight inches square, Meg thought with trepidation.

Livy noted the measurements on a sheet of paper.

They went to the left side of the door and repeated their measurement of the width. "The wall on this side is about half a foot less wide, same height."

"I have it."

"The five flat columns are each sixteen inches wide. They will be easier, and I can start with them. I'll paint the countess's roses twining up a trellis." The designs for the small spaces took shape in Meg's mind as she spoke.

"Here they are, already at work." Sutton rolled Lady Wakefield's bath chair into the conservatory, followed by a cadre of footmen with four chairs, a table, and a velvet-covered chaise.

"My, gels, I admire your diligence so early in the morning. I presume you have eaten breakfast, but I have not. Over here, Elliot," the countess directed a footman.

In a twinkling the bare simplicity of the room was transformed. Sutton supervised the placement of the furniture, and Elliott set a tea tray on the table.

"Mr. Ames should be along any moment," the countess rattled on. "Miss Hayward, while I am thinking about measuring, please run up to my boudoir and find my maid, Hartley. She is ready to alter one of my old riding habits for you. It won't be the first stare of fashion, but at least you will be appropriately dressed when you ride."

"But, my lady, I will be quite occupied right here. I hardly need—"

"No arguments, missy. Run along now, and hurry back for your chocolate." The countess waved her beringed fingers at Meg as if whisking away a pesky gnat.

Without further argument, Meg found her way upstairs to Hartley, a briskly efficient female who pinched, poked, twisted, and turned Meg so quickly, she was almost dizzy. The burgundy color of the habit appealed to her, but Hartley's fingers flew so fast, pinning, tucking, and turning each piece inside out that she never saw the outside of the jacket. Its style remained a mystery.

When Meg returned to the conservatory, Lord Wakefield and a strange man, apparently Mr. Ames, had joined Livy and the countess, who reclined gracefully on her chaise, reminding Meg of an etching portraying a Roman empress at a banquet. Meg avoided looking directly at Lord Wakefield, but a furtive quick glance had disclosed pearl-gray breeches and a dark blue coat, an ensemble even more appealing than the one he wore last evening.

"Mr. Ames agrees the walls ought to be covered

with canvas before you start your painting," the countess announced.

"I can acquire the proper-weight material in a day
or two and apply it later this week, if that is satisfac-
tory, my lady."

"Have you anything to add, Miss Hayward?" the
countess asked.

Meg felt her sense of apprehension growing. "I, ah,
I will need a primer coat, will I not, Mr. Ames?"

"My man can do that for you if you wish, and leave
the surface all ready for you."

"And can you supply me with the pigments?"

"It would be my pleasure," Mr. Ames said with a
smile.

"Thank you." At least she could trust him to give
her the proper type of paints. Obviously simple watercolors would never do.

The earl escorted Mr. Ames back into the house
after the company exchanged appropriate adieus.

The countess poured herself another cup of tea, add-
ing a few drops of cream. "That was very simple. And
by the time we have completed our nuncheon, the
roads will have dried out sufficiently for your little
jaunt to town."

Meg's pleasure at concluding the conversation without revealing her appalling ignorance of mural painting was dashed when she noticed sunshine had
replaced the rain.

"Your dear sister has agreed to read to me as I enjoy
my very first afternoon in my conservatory."

Meg looked helplessly at Livy, whose face remained
blandly innocent. Somehow Meg was going to have to
endure several hours alone in the company of that
rogue. Perhaps she ought to keep a nice sharp, hat pin

handy, in case their conversational exchanges once more became too personal.

Lord Wakefield was all that was proper as he handed Meg into his open phaeton. Meg composed her face into what she intended to be a primly pleasant countenance. She would make no more impertinent remarks. The money earned from her painting had to be her highest consideration. If the earl wished to amuse himself by teasing her, Meg would ignore his efforts. Or at the very least, try to maintain her dignity.

One of Papa's old books said it best. "Knowledge is power," wrote Sir Francis Bacon centuries ago. Now Meg intended to learn as much as she could about the earl. And her aim had a second useful attribute: She was certain the earl would enjoy discussing nothing so much as himself. The subject should occupy every moment of their journey.

Feeling not a little smug in her command of the situation, Meg looked over the equipage in which she waited. One could have expected no less from Lord High-and-Haughty. Leather, brass, horseflesh—indeed every surface gleamed. The young tiger stood at attention while the earl conferred with his steward on the steps leading to the old Hall. Not even the horses dared to stamp in impatience.

Drat the man. Lord Wakefield was perfectly turned out, as always, with not a thread out of place. As she watched, he fitted flawless gloves over his long fingers and smoothed them across his palms, his movements as graceful as they were casual. His gray hat, of precisely the same shade as his gloves and waistcoat, sat atop his dark curls at the exact angle to declare his distinction yet give notice of the ease with which he carried it.

Lord Wakefield shook hands with the steward and nodded to Sutton, who waited at the door. So far, Meg thought, he has been exceedingly considerate of his servants, not a quality she ordinarily associated with his ilk. And one had to admit he doted upon his grandmother. The countess attributed the construction of her conservatory entirely to his insistence on her ease and enjoyment.

After a quick check of the matched chestnuts and a few words to each horse, Lord Wakefield put an arm around the shoulder of the young tiger. "Hop aboard, Benjamin," he said, and swung up beside Meg. He picked up the reins, nodded to the groom, and spoke to the team. "Walk on."

As they rolled down the drive, Meg turned to look at the house, or castle as it appeared from this angle. She was surprised to note the flutter of a silk curtain at a first-floor window. Who would have been watching their departure? She shrugged a little and settled herself for the trip.

"Are you familiar with Berkshire, Miss Hayward?" the earl asked.

"I am afraid not. The visit to London was my first venture beyond the borders of Sussex since I was ten years old. Did you grow up at Wakefield Hall?"

"I was born here but spent more time at my father's much-smaller holding in Hampshire. I came to Wakefield at Christmas, of course. As a matter of fact, when I was a boy, I seem to have spent more time at school than anyplace else."

Meg wondered if the wistfulness she detected in his

tone was merely her imagination. "Did you attend Eton?"

"Yes, and after that a few years at Oxford before the army."

"Did you serve in Portugal?"

"No, though I tried to get there several times. I am afraid my service was confined to the coastal fortifications in Kent."

They turned out of the drive between tall stone pillars, leaving behind the sweeping lawns and clusters of trees of the park. Over their heads, the gentle greens of the newly leafed trees formed a canopy, pierced by shafts of sunlight.

"Why did you leave the army?" Meg asked.

"I had hoped to tell you a bit about the countryside, rather than succumb to an interrogation, Miss Hayward."

The hint of irony in his voice annoyed her. "I beg your pardon, my lord. Please proceed with your lesson."

To Meg's surprise, he laughed out loud. "I fear we shall soon be back to goading each other, which has landed me in difficulty in our previous conversations. I propose we choose a neutral topic, Miss Hayward."

"I assure you, I quite fancy your commentary on the Berkshire countryside, Lord Wakefield. In fact, nothing would please me more." At least she could develop a few ideas for her paintings.

"Pray excuse me if I deem that a slight exaggeration. However, I will point out these magnificent stands of beech that seem to thrive on our chalky soil and the nearness of the Thames. One of my grandmama's greatest regrets is that she no longer can wander in the beech forests to find the delicate little

orchids that bloom in the deep woods in the spring.
They are golden brown in color, called Birdsnest Orchids, and she loved the annual excursions when they
bloomed."

"Are they in bloom now? I should like to sketch
them, perhaps to include on one of the walls."

"Soon, if not now. I have not actually seen them for
years." He paused for a moment, then continued.
"Most of the area has been in wheat and barley fields
since prehistoric men first left evidence of their presence. And grazing land, too. In medieval times, of
course, the economy was based on sheep farming and
the wool trade."

"And today?"

"Much the same. Mostly, we grow wheat on the
estate, though we have both dairy and beef herds as
well as five distinct breeds of sheep."

Meg was beginning to visualize a sweeping view of
meadowlands dotted with animals, a wheat field, and
a patch of beech forest on the walls.

The phaeton crossed an ancient stone bridge over a
fast-running stream, which curved to parallel their
path. A blanket of wildflowers covered the edge of the
road and the banks of the stream. Pink bramble roses
honored the morning rainfall by turning their bright
faces to the sunny sky, along with blue pasqueflowers
and columbines in every shade of purple.

Lord Wakefield slowed the horses to a walk as they
approached the village. Whitewashed cottages with
dark oak beams and thickly thatched roofs lined the
street, many with colorful flower boxes at their windows. A moss-covered wall set off the churchyard and
the square Norman tower of All Souls Church. The

village green was dotted with flowering trees and bright beds of yellow primroses.

Everywhere she looked, Meg found ideas and inspiration for her wall paintings. To the meadow and forest scene, she now could add a tumbling brook, a quaint village with picturesque church and green.

"We will not stop here for the moment, Miss Hayward. A few more minutes will bring us to Wallingford, where the shops will have a better selection."

"Whatever you say, my lord."

The grays picked up speed as they passed the last house in the village. The road now ran along the riverbank.

"Is this the Thames, Lord Wakefield?"

"Yes, upstream, Father Thames runs past Oxford and downstream to Windsor, then on to London. Wallingford gained its first importance as a shallow crossing point long before the Romans arrived."

"Then it must be very old."

"Indeed, though little is left from the prerestoration days. The medieval plagues nearly emptied the town, and its fortifications were virtually leveled by Cromwell. But you will nevertheless find it a pleasant spot with all the amenities of a market town." As the horses trotted briskly along, the earl continued his commentary on local affairs.

By the time they reached the high street, Meg felt as though she knew more about this corner of Berkshire than she did about her own home district in Sussex.

"You have been an attentive listener, Miss Hayward," Nicholas said. "I hope I have not bored you with too many obscure historical details."

Meg flashed him her most winning smile. "I have

found your discourse quite engrossing, and I thank you for your eloquence."

"Ah, that's a bit thick." He looked at her with quizzically raised eyebrows.

Meg could hardly squelch her urge to giggle. "If you do not care to listen to my toad-eating, then we should proceed with our missions."

"I shall accompany you to the stationer to establish your right to use my accounts." He handed her down from the phaeton and tossed the reins to Benjamin.

A half hour later, their packages sent to the carriage, Lord Wakefield assigned Benjamin to follow Miss Hayward as she perused the other delights of the high street. "I have several people to see, then I shall meet you at the coffee room of the George in about an hour," Lord Wakefield said.

Meg could tell from Benjamin's solemn stance that he took his responsibilities seriously. With a little smile at the sturdy lad, she headed for the bow window of Madame Beaufort, milliner.

Nicholas paused at the corner and looked back to satisfy himself Miss Hayward would be secure. With Benjamin standing behind her, she had practically pressed her nose against the glass of the town's premier hat shop. She was grasping the worn ribbons of her straw bonnet, an article that obviously had served more than its share of summers. How he would love to see her go into Madame Beaufort's and try on candidates for replacement. He could see her in his mind's eye, turning and preening before the looking glass, first a tall poke bonnet with sweeping feathers, then a frothy confection of pink silk roses. Her eyes would be wide with excitement and perhaps even amazement as she caught a glimpse of how lovely she was.

But she turned from the shop and continued away from him down the high street. Quickly he brought himself back to reality and hurried off to meet his local solicitor about his plans to acquire acreage adjoining the western boundary of Wakefield.

By the time he arrived at the George, he was a quarter hour late, and he feared she would be upset. Instead, she bent over a small booklet, intensely concentrating on its content.

"Miss Hayward, please excuse my tardiness," he said, sitting down across a low table from her.

She looked up with surprise evident in her eyes. "I had no idea it was past time for you. I have been quite absorbed in this little volume I found in the book stall."

He read the title as she held it up before her. *"A Short History of Wallingford and Vicinity, Being a Treatise on Royal Connexions, Famous Men and Distinguished Edifices of N. Berkshire."* Nicholas could not suppress his smile.

"Then you were not bamming me when you said you wanted to know more," he said.

"Perhaps I am merely corroborating your stories," she replied with a saucy toss of her head.

"You shall find my version to be precise and entirely factual." He used his most haughty tone, then leaned close to her and whispered. "If, that is, my memory has not entirely failed me."

"So far, you deserve only my accolades for accuracy."

His twinge of satisfaction at her praise startled the earl. Why was he in any way affected by her little tribute?

The proprietor of the George hovered at the earl's

elbow. "Good day, my lord. What may I serve you today?"

Once he had given the orders and their glasses were on the table, Miss Hayward tucked the booklet into a paper parcel containing her purchases.

"Would I be prying if I asked what caught your fancy?" he asked.

"Not at all, sir. But you must promise to keep this a secret. I have a small piece of silk and a few scraps of lace and ribbon for Livy. While I paint, she has in mind to stitch a few sachets for your grandmama. Above all, we want to do something to show our appreciation for her kindness."

"I shall keep your confidence. The countess is often lonely, I fear. She will enjoy the company of young ladies enough to negate the need for any tokens of thanks, but I understand the gesture and I approve."

Miss Hayward almost choked on her lemonade. "How very gracious of you, my lord," she sputtered.

He grinned and shook his head. "All right, Miss Hayward, I know you think I sound like a pompous ass, and you are probably correct."

"You see, Lord Wakefield, the very mischievous light in your eyes belies the priggish nature of your words. Something is quite out of whack between your inner character and your outward demeanor, I suspect."

"You don't say."

"Yes, and this is not the first time I have noticed your difficulty in acting like a proper earl when you long to be otherwise."

Nicholas wondered if his neckcloth had gone awry or if he had slopped lemonade on his lapel. But apparently the little minx had more insight than he guessed.""Perhaps your imagination is more vividly alive than you realize."

"Imagination? I seem to recall a few remarks—"

"Please, Miss Hayward, I have confessed my lapse of good conduct, and I readily beg your indulgence again."

"Not just *that* remark, Lord Wakefield."

He rolled his eyes to the low-beamed ceiling and tented his fingers. "Dare I continue this most distressing conversation? Ah, I think I pursue the allegations at my own substantial risk." He lowered his eyes to meet hers. "Shall we collect the phaeton, Miss Hayward?"

"As you wish, Lord Wakefield." Meg stood and walked briskly toward the door as the earl handed coins to the proprietor and wished him good day.

Nicholas was far more amused than he dared acknowledge. Miss Hayward was quite a rare find, a worthy companion for his grandmama indeed. He found himself looking forward to the carriage ride back to Wakefield with particular relish.

Miss Hayward looked about with lively interest as their carriage passed down the high street. He watched as she craned her neck to take in every shop.

"Livy will enjoy visiting these shops one day," she said.

"You and your sister enjoy great mutual harmony."

"Yes, we are very close."

"And the others in your family?"

"I have two more sisters, Pandora and Beatrice, my lord, ages fifteen and sixteen, both very beautiful and clever beyond their years. My father's sisters also reside with us, but sadly Aunt Alice is prey to a wandering of the mind, and her fate is a sad trial to Aunt Regina."

"And what of your parents, Miss Hayward?"

"My mother is dead these twelve years and my father leads a very reclusive life. He was once devoted to his scientific experiments, though I regret he did not make any significant progress toward fulfilling his dream."

"And that is?"

"He was engaged in developing a process for removing salt from seawater. It was his life's work, and though he can distill small amounts of pure water, a method of increasing the volume of his achievement eludes him."

"How disappointing." Nicholas could not help feeling pity for the man. How frustrating his work must have been in such a futile quest.

"Yes, he was certain his success would materially change the fortunes of the navy, among other advances all across the realm."

"I daresay he was correct."

"However, as a practical matter, his work at least provided us with an ample supply of sea salt for the kitchen." She gave an ironic shrug. "Now I fear he drifts far from reality most of the time."

Nicholas wished he had a quick change of subject at hand, for he couldn't help feeling a touch of melancholy at the thought of the elderly scientist's disappointment and that of his daughter.

"If I may be so bold as to ask a question regarding finances, my lord?" Miss Hayward asked.

He nodded, puzzled at what she might be about to mention.

"Have you any experience with investing, as in buying consols or shares on the Exchange?"

Nicholas couldn't have been more surprised if she had asked him the source of his smallclothes. "A bit. Why ever would that subject interest you?"

"As you no doubt have guessed, Lord Wakefield, the Hayward family is without a steady source of income. I have managed to save a small amount, which I would like to put to work. I know little of such doings, but I know it is possible to increase one's funds over a period of time by entrusting those funds to a successful venture. It is a very small amount, just about a hundred pounds," she was quick to add. "But it could enable Pandora and Beatrice to have a turn in London when the time arrives."

"Ah, so you want to provide for your sisters' comeouts?" he asked.

"Exactly. They deserve the opportunity to see and be seen."

So, he thought, it was the London marriage mart she had in mind for her sisters. Strange she should not consider her own future.

"Why not a few pounds for your own benefit, Miss Hayward?"

"Ah, my lord, someone has to care for Father and the aunts. Livy and I have a dream every bit as dear to us as father's was to him. Our wish is to see our younger sisters happily wed. Livy and I shall muddle along, enjoying our quiet life with the others."

What she meant, Nicholas thought, was she and Livy would endure a life of spinsterhood in order to care for the eccentric father and the batty old aunts, a noble choice, perhaps, but hardly fair. Miss Hayward had much too much verve to moulder away in the depths of Sussex.

"Of course, Miss Hayward, it is also possible to buy shares in a venture which fails, as many have. Then your money would be gone forever."

"And that, my lord, is why I seek your advice."

"Let me give it some thought. My man of business has proven astute in the past, and I shall seek his counsel."

"Thank you, Lord Wakefield." Meg seemed suddenly embarrassed and shy, turning her gaze to the passing countryside.

He liked her better when she was on her toes, parrying his every provocation with a witty rejoinder. "And how did you acquire your original stake, Miss Hayward? Perhaps a market in *faux* antique items, such as French china or, perhaps, fans?"

Her head whipped around, mouth wide and eyes flashing. "Why, now that you mention it, I suppose I shall have to admit to a thriving traffic in smuggled French spirits. Indeed, why should I stoop to frilly items for milady's delight when I can provide the exact object of every English nobleman's desire. One can certainly be assured that few fine residences, whether in London or in the country, lack the exceptional product of our perfidious enemy's vineyards."

Lord Wakefield laughed heartily at her outburst. "Oh, capital, Miss Hayward! I am indeed delighted to have made your acquaintance, for having a select source for French brandy is my fondest wish. Please arrange for several barrels to be sent to Wakefield immediately." The earl handed her the reins as he sought in his pocket for a handkerchief with which to wipe his eyes.

"You don't have to choke yourself, my lord. It was hardly that amusing."

The thought of the petite Miss Hayward hefting huge barrels on her pretty shoulder brought Nicholas another burst of laughter.

"My lord, I am not known as a fine whip," Meg admonished. "You have entrusted your excellent pair to one who is accustomed to driving only a plebeian donkey cart."

Lord Wakefield's imagination shifted to a picture of Miss Hayward driving a donkey cart full of brandy along the Channel beach. When he somewhat recovered his aplomb, he watched the horses for a moment. "The chestnuts are tooling along perfectly. You have steady hands, Miss Hayward."

"Naturellement, monsieur," she drawled in a heavy French accent. "Ze donkee, he is *très* sensitive and ze *fumé de* brandee, they wobble him *à facile.*"

Chuckling, Lord Wakefield shook his head. "I suggest your primary investment ought to be in more donkeys, the better to move those contraband spirits."

Never taking her eyes off the horses, Miss Hayward sniffed in disdain. "Believe me, Lord Wakefield, the thought of smuggling as a career is more tempting to me than you could possibly imagine. The potential of the *faux* antique business pales in comparison."

"Miss Hayward, you have made me laugh, something I have missed in recent days." Nicholas hadn't been so entertained in a very long time, and probably never by a female other than his grandmama.

Miss Hayward stared at the horses, her lips set in a determined line. The usual curls escaped from her bonnet to quiver in the breeze, but instead of looking disheveled he found her perfectly adorable. As he watched, she turned her head a little to take a quick glance in his direction, and broke into a little giggle that quickly turned to outright laughter as he joined in.

"You need more laughter in your life, my lord."

"Perhaps I do." He felt amazingly lighthearted; he had so many serious concerns to deal with, he had neglected his own pleasures. Miss Hayward was like a fresh breeze on a sultry day.

"But," she added, "if you laugh at me, do not forget that we unprincipled swindlers have many nefarious methods of exacting our revenge."

Yes, he thought as he took the reins back from Miss Hayward, and one of those methods might be to challenge my resolve. I must be vigilant not to succumb to the kind of romantic notions I have always despised.

Five

Meg sat in the silent conservatory, an empty sketch-pad on her knees. Yesterday's rosy outlook had dis-solved into the depths of last night's sleeplessness. Now her head was filled with shifting scenes and rap-idly differing images, transforming themselves before she could place a single line on the page. The village church, the fields, the pattern of trees bled into a rain-bow of colors, leaving her nothing she could picture clearly. Yesterday, with the beauty of the district un-folding around her, she had presumed her work could proceed without impediment. Today she saw naught but blank white paper and blank white walls, barren and empty, as desolate as her brain.

The old worries returned triplefold. And soon, she thought, surveying the chaise and the circle of unoc-cupied chairs, Livy and the countess would arrive to observe her despair. No, her doubts and fears were not to share with anybody. Fortunately she had her shawl and a small sketchbook, and with these in hand, she quietly let herself out of the conservatory by the gar-den door.

Perhaps she could sketch some rosebuds or trailing vines of the wisteria, anything to abolish her appalling lack of inspiration. In the carriage, while trading ob-servations with Lord Wakefield, she easily visualized the passing landscape captured on the wall. Where had her creativity gone? Hiding in the thorns of humiliation over her reaction to the earl? He was so awfully attractive. For a few isolated moments now and then she had enjoyed his company. From time to time the man acted like a human being instead of a stiff monument to English rectitude. She admired the way his eyes gleamed with pride in his land, and his smile brought cheer to the faces of those he addressed. His very voice promised a strength and virility that made her knees weak.

She sank onto a stone bench and applied herself to rendering the shape of a rose in the middle of the page. This was no time to shilly-shally. She should get to work before she generated some impossible tendresse for Lord Wakefield. He should mean nothing to her, not even an object of her private dreams. She didn't have to worry if he didn't like the paintings, as long as her work satisfied his grandmama.

Meg extended the stem of the rose and added two clusters of leaves dotted with dewdrops. Maybe a few confidence-building sessions like this would give her courage. The drawing was nothing special, but neither was it atrocious. She turned the page and tried to portray the path and trellis at its end, a little exercise in perspective. Every day she wasted was one more day for temptation and one day farther from going home.

Nicholas breakfasted with his grandmama and Livy, who virtually ignored his presence. They discussed their mutual preference for the music of the harpsichord, which, he gathered, Livy played, rather than the more modern fortepiano.

He concentrated on his tasks for the morning and his best approach to Squire Grennan. As he had explained the previous day to his solicitor, the land had lain fallow for a decade or more, subject to frequent flooding from the brook Nicholas planned to divert half a mile away.

"Nicky?"

He shook himself from his reverie. "Why, Grandmama, you noticed my presence at last."

"Yes, I did, and I have a favor to ask of you."

"Today may be difficult. I need to ride over to Grennan's."

"You can do that any day. Who knows how long the bluebells will be out?"

"What?"

"Miss Hayward apparently has been up for some time. Please find her and ride down to the lake so that she can see the fields in full bloom. Last evening when she talked of her interest in our verdure, I immediately remembered the most pleasing vista on the estate."

"Perhaps tomorrow I could accompany her to the lake."

"Tomorrow it might rain. I will have Hartley hang the riding habit in her room immediately." She gestured his dismissal.

Nicholas shook his head. "Grandmama, you must see that my business is very important. I told you about my hope to—"

"Bosh! Old Grennan will talk your ears off and make you come back five times before he consents. If I were you, I would postpone meeting him as long as possible."

He shook his head. "I suppose I will never hear the

end of it if I don't follow your very high-handed orders, Grandmama."

"High-handed indeed! I am merely thinking of your best interests."

"And I am the Sultan of Morocco! As always, my dearest Grandmama, you win."

"Why thank you, Sir Sultan."

Nicholas had to admit the grin on her face made him glad. And actually, Grandmama's request met his urgent wish to see how well Miss Hayward handled the mare he had chosen for her to ride. If her skills proved tolerable, he could send her on sketching expeditions with his tiger, Benjamin. Nicholas had no need to spend more time with Miss Hayward. Yesterday, on the trip to Wallingford, she had been quite amusing and certainly easy on his eyes. But despite her comic tales, he still wondered just how capable she would be as a muralist. Further, the countess might be subject to devious manipulation by Miss Olivia, who seemed to be ingratiating herself deeply into the lonely old lady's confidence. In the light of the morning, he felt embarrassed at his easy familiarity with Miss Hayward yesterday. From now on, he had to keep himself under better control while keeping his eye on those two young ladies.

After today, he could do that at a distance. He needed something to insulate himself from daily contact with them, a reason to be away from the Hall on most days.

In the meantime, the conservatory decoration was his grandmama's project, and the young ladies were her concern. His duties were elsewhere on the estate. Beginning tomorrow, he had no intention of spending time in their company.

On the other hand, he might be making something out of nothing at all. *Stop this damn swerving back and forth, Wakefield!* He was rapidly becoming as missish as an old maid!

After an exasperating search, he found the so-called artist in the garden, around a corner, out of view of the house.

"Miss Hayward." He made an attempt to keep his voice quiet and controlled.

"Over here."

"Good morning." He greeted her with a bow and a half smile. "The countess is impatient to know your whereabouts. She has a suggestion for your activities today."

Meg continued to draw, giving him only a quick glance before she tipped the paper pad away from his view. "Please go on."

"Since the day is so fine, she wishes us to ride to the lake. The field of bluebells should be in full bloom. While you sketch, I can see if the Birdsnest Orchids are out yet."

Meg frowned. "I have tried to tell you, my lord, but you have not heard me. My experience in the saddle was many, many years ago. I fear that even with the fine riding clothes the countess was kind enough to provide, I would have a very difficult time going anywhere on horseback."

"Riding is one of those skills you can hardly forget. I have a perfect mount for you, a very gentle mare you are sure to enjoy."

"But, I really don't think . . ." Her voice trailed off.

"You are a game girl, Miss Hayward. No sense in procrastinating . . ." He felt so irritable, he wished he could give her a good hard shake.

"Surely you have other duties."

"Nothing that cannot wait a few hours. I am accustomed to riding most mornings anyway."

He watched her consider her alternatives. Her every sensibility flashed onto her face, reflected in the deepening pink of her cheeks, the tilt of her head, the cast of her mouth, the glint in her eye. He could see her slowly begin to modify her opposition to the excursion. From defiance, she apparently moved toward agreement, as her chin raised and her frown lightened. With an expressive face like hers, being a liar and schemer must be doubly difficult. Again he was reminded what a most unlikely criminal she seemed. But schemer she was, and before she left, he would prove it to his grandmama.

Almost an hour later, he waited with the horses at the front steps, wondering if the jaunt all the way to the lake was a wise effort. Miss Hayward probably ought to try a turn around the paddock for a day or two in order to grow accustomed to the mare. But all his thoughts of safety were wiped away when she appeared, a charming picture framed by the door. The deep burgundy habit flattered her trim figure. Its tight jacket and the sweeping skirt gave her a deceptively imposing stature. The jaunty little hat, perched on her upswept curls, supported several fluffy white feathers. Her frown of apprehension could pass for the jaded expression of a patrician lady of refinement. Gone entirely was the rural miss whose hair never minded its ribbon, whose outdated gown was so modest as to be rustic.

Her gaze focused on the quiet chestnut mare held by Benjamin. Nicholas stifled a smile at the adoration on the face of the young tiger as he beheld the new magnificence of Miss Hayward. Now she looked like a female quite capable of gulling anyone. Or charming a dozen London dandies for that matter.

"This is Sunbeam, a very sweet-tempered mount," Lord Wakefield said. "Come, give her a piece of carrot."

Miss Hayward gathered the long skirt and stepped hesitantly toward them. "What is your horse called, my lord?"

"He is Diamond Dust." Nicholas placed the carrot in her hand.

She wrinkled her nose and shut her eyes as she extended the treat to the horse.

"It is best to hold your hand flat. You do not want her to nip your fingers."

"Yes, of course," she muttered, and opened her eyes as well as her palm. "Nice Sunbeam."

The mare took the carrot and crunched noisily.

Lord Wakefield smiled. "Table manners are not her most admirable quality. Here, now, I will give you a toss up."

Before she could change her mind, he lifted her into the saddle. Her lightness surprised him and his fingers tingled at the contact with her warmth, his hand lingering at her waist for an instant before he adjusted her stirrup. She wriggled around a little before settling into position and picking up the reins.

"Are you comfortable?"

"As much as I can be up here. I do remember how to sit, but I do not remember being so high."

"I will lead her if you wish."

"Certainly not. I shall manage on my own."

Glad to distance himself from her, Nicholas mounted his impatient gray and waved Ben to release the mare. Dusty was eager for a good gallop, dancing forty steps for every one of the mare's, but the earl kept to a sedate pace. He tried to watch Miss Hayward without being too obvious.

She held her head high and back straight, whether with the stiffness of fear or as correct riding posture he wasn't sure. Her brow was still creased, in concentration he assumed, and her lips pursed in a rosebud of diligent concern. He was pleased to see how her hands were easy on the reins, responding to the natural bobbing motion of the mare's head.

"Are you beginning to feel secure, Miss Hayward?" he asked.

"Hardly that. But I am coping, my lord."

"And very well, I must say. It does not appear to have been a long time since you were frequently in the saddle."

"Something close to twelve years. When my mama was alive, we kept saddle horses. She was a bruising rider."

He waited for more, but she was silent. Her life must have altered dramatically when her mother died. As oldest daughter she probably bore the weight of all the family's trials. Apparently she still did. Such devotion surely deserved great admiration. Family burdens could be difficult. For him, such duty brought tremendous reward. Then again, he was not saddled with a houseful of dependents, many of them without a full complement of sense. Whatever income the Hayward family had once enjoyed, it now appeared to be next to nothing. Ah, except that hundred pounds about which she needed his advice.

"Perhaps we could try a little jog?" he asked.

"A very, very little jog."

He allowed Diamond Dust to direct his prancing steps forward instead of from side to side. The mare picked up her pace to keep stride. Miss Hayward winced at the jostling she received from the bouncing gait, but she soon adjusted her movements to the rhythm of her mount. Indeed, she remembered, even if she did not realize how or why.

"Very good, Miss Hayward. Are you sure you have not been out practicing?"

"Quite, my lord. I dare not look down, even now."

But Nicholas could see she had the horse under control. Perhaps tomorrow he would even try her at a slow canter. If she handled that competently, he would have no fear sending her off alone, except for Ben. Though perhaps he pushed her too fast. It would be quite rude of him to abandon her too quickly.

"How are you getting along, Miss Hayward?"

"A bit better, Lord Wakefield. To tell the truth, I am beginning to enjoy myself. Do you think we could try a little gallop. I seem to remember that gait was more comfortable than this trot."

"At your service," he replied, giving the signal to the gray. Hearing Miss Hayward cluck to Sunbeam, he looked around. The broad smile on Miss Hayward's face as she leaned into the rocking motion of the canter astounded him with its loveliness.

"Why, I think I do recall more than I ever assumed I would," she called.

Nicholas could not imagine why he felt a stab of disappointment rather than relief.

Meg enjoyed the breeze fanning her cheeks, the cadence of the horses' hooves, and the feeling of power coursing through her. If Lord Wakefield's presence had not been so obviously, so gloriously male, she would have thought herself returned to those happy days when she followed her mother across the Downs at a daring speed. Meg threw back her head and laughed out loud. Whatever would her life be when she returned to Sussex and that plodding donkey?

In no more than ten minutes, they slowed again to a walk.

"Just through these trees, you will see the slope toward the lake," Lord Wakefield announced.

As Sunbeam carried her through a narrow stand of trees, Meg watched the sun slide from behind a cloud, flooding the woods with light gently filtered through the pale young leaves. Along the lake, a carpet of bluebells spread to the water's edge. The violet-blue glowed vividly against the lichened gray stones of a small bridge. On the hillside beyond, three lambs cavorted, their youthful activity a sharp contrast to the placid bulks of their grazing mamas.

The scene utterly captivated Meg. "I know why this is one of your grandmama's favorite places." Her voice was barely more than a whisper.

"Sad to say, she cannot get here anymore."

"Will the bluebells grow in the conservatory?"

"I hope so, though of course the effect of a whole hillside of blue cannot be reproduced."

"Except on the wall." She turned the mare back toward the trees. She needed to find the perfect vista for her sketches.

In a matter of minutes she was established on a rug with her pencils and sketchbook, while Lord Wakefield led the horses away. Meg arranged the velvet skirt around her in a graceful circle, letting her fingertips caress the soft fabric before she turned her attention to her work.

Faced with the beauty of the landscape, not a trace of her early-morning hesitancy lingered. The distant hillside was crowned with trees, the slope downward to the lake dotted with sheep. As she sketched the characteristic arch of the bridge, the earl brought the horses to drink at the lake. Without thinking, she deftly added them to the scene. They were too far away to be more than a few lines, but she lingered over his image for a long time.

Though her pencil continued to move over the page, placing a rock here, a flock of sheep there, Lord Wakefield's earlier look of astonishment occupied Meg's thoughts. That morning, before he noticed her standing on the steps outside the hall, he had worn his usual mask of polite disinterest. The sudden change, his widened eyes, and quick smile made her feel all soft and melting inside, even now, as she merely recalled the moment. Of course, his surprise at her appearance was due to the lovely habit and to the elegant hairstyle Hartley created with Lady Wakefield's guidance.

Meg wished she knew how to interpret the earl's attitudes. She had looked away quickly to hide her lack of composure. Then outright fear of the horse had driven everything else from her mind. Funny, now, an hour later, she was rather comfortable with the horse, but the man's expression still bothered her.

Knowing little of the ladies of the *ton,* she wondered how he looked at other females. Certainly many pursued him. A handsome earl with a substantial fortune would be a catch for anyone, even a duke's daughter. Meg outlined a few clouds above the hill and darkened the shadows of a grove of trees on the distant hill.

Lord Wakefield hobbled the horses in the grass beyond the bluebells, then walked over to peer at her work.

"Quite admirable, Miss Hayward," he said. "You have caught the sweep of those hills exactly."

"Thank you."

"If you are comfortable here, with Ben keeping an eye on the horses, I will walk into the woods and see if I can find any trace of those little orchids."

"I am quite content, my lord. I have many objects to draw, from the petals of the flower to the twisted limbs of those trees." She gazed at him with a new awareness. His face formed an oval embellished by the smooth planes of his cheeks, strong dark brows . . .

"Then I shall return shortly."

When he was a few yards away, she flipped to a clean sheet and squeezed her eyes shut. There was his face, his lips, the frame of his dark hair . . .

The minutes sped by as Meg covered that sheet and several more with quick sketches of his face, his profile, his tall figure. When she heard his whistle from afar, she quickly found another blank sheet and leaned down close to produce a few very close renditions of the frilly blue blossoms and their slender stalks. She drew rapidly, a different angle for each one, not taking an instant to check his progress.

"We are in luck," the earl announced, then knelt beside her. "Even in just the gray of the pencil, I would recognize these flowers anywhere. When you add color, they will be splendid."

"I hope so."

"The orchids are a very little distance from us. May I show you?"

"Please do." Meg took his hand and rose to her feet,

shaking out the long skirt and tucking her pad tightly under her arm. She certainly didn't want him to browse through the drawings. She would be embarrassed beyond imagination if he saw the ones of himself.

In the woods, the ancient beech trees seemed as old as England itself. A pungent aroma wafted out of the carpet of damp leaves beneath their feet. The ground was spongy, with moss and ferns growing in the narrow shafts of sunlight that pierced the dense canopy of leaves. The songs of the warblers had an echoing quality, as though they sang from the choir of a towering old cathedral.

"Over here." Lord Wakefield knelt near the broad base of an ancient beech.

Meg crouched down to view fragile curling stalks of pale beige with tiny fringed flowers. The Birdsnest Orchids were different from the enormous exotic purple varieties imported from far-off jungles. These looked ethereal, like the creations of the little people, the ancient ones who knew the magic of these forests and formed these diminutive nests for the miniature creatures that inhabited their enchanted land.

Lord Wakefield spread his jacket on the leaves so she could sit, and she opened her sketchbook to a blank page, folding the other sheets underneath.

Lord Wakefield strolled around the little glen while she drew, fading from her consciousness as she concentrated on capturing the delicacy of the minute blooms. As if to belie their inconsequential size, each little stalk thrust up through layers of leaves from the moist loam beneath. High overhead the sun winked through the pale young leaves, so very far in color, texture, and weight from those now sheltering the little orchids.

If only she had her watercolors to help her capture the tints here in this strange and wonderful place. Instead, she would have to rely on her memory. The soft cream of the stems with streaks of pale green, the dark feathering at the ends. She leaned over to see more closely, breathing the musty scent of the rich earth. These were secret orchids, hidden from the view of anyone who did not seek them out. Though she detected no scent from the orchids themselves, she felt almost light-headed, as though they drew her into their own mysterious world.

The earl's returning footsteps rustled the top layer of dry beech leaves, and he knelt beside her, wordless, perhaps caught in those same unusual sensations she felt, so curious, so entrancing. The moment stretched into an eternity, silent except for their breathing.

At last Lord Wakefield moved away. "They are odd little plants, are they not?"

Meg sat back on his jacket. "I almost expect to see a fairy dancing beside them."

She couldn't tell if his reaction was a half-laugh or a sniff of censure. "I think a beetle or some winged insect would be far more likely. How did your sketches turn out?"

She held them up and he crouched down again, studying the drawings she held. "Very realistic, very detailed." His surprise was evident in his tone.

"You think they are good likenesses?"

"You capture so much with just a few lines."

He was so very close, nearly touching her shoulder, his cheek only inches from hers. Meg's heart pounded unexplainably as he lifted her hand and turned it over, intertwining his fingers with hers. He raised it to his mouth and touched the back of her hand with his lips, then turned it over and kissed her palm.

Deep within her, Meg felt a warmth invade her innermost being, a series of tingles dance along her nerves. She dared not move, dared not breathe.

With his thumb, he caressed her jaw, then turned her chin toward him and very slowly, very softly touched her lips with his.

"Miss Hayward, you have a most unusual effect upon me."

Meg expected anger to grasp her, but instead she wished he would kiss her again. Her body felt all trembly inside, and she was helpless to stop it. She said nothing but stared into his eyes for a moment. His power was far more potent than the orchid's beauty.

Abruptly he stood. "I seem to need to apologize every time I am with you for more than three minutes."

Just as suddenly, a stab of rage flashed alive in Meg. She refused to allow him to trifle with her. Earl or no earl, he had no right to treat her as a novelty for his amusement. "Oh, I see. That your behavior is so reprehensible is the result of *my* effect on you. What a very convenient way to absolve yourself from blame, Lord Wakefield."

He frowned sharply. "You have twisted my words and distorted my meaning. I refuse to become involved in a word game. I will bring the horses." He stalked away, even from behind the image of annoyance.

She fought back the tear that seemed to come from nowhere and leaned closer to the tiny flowers, resettling her drawing pad and trying to sketch from a different angle. The more she thought about it, the more indignant she became until she realized she had sketched little frowning faces on several of her flowers.

Yet her lips still tingled and her heartbeat raced. His lips had been so very soft, his touch so very gentle. What she wanted to abhor she instead wished to experience again. And again.

Six

Once at the entrance of Wakefield Hall, Meg slid off the mare, fumbling with her drawing pad, pencil case, and the heavy folds of her long velvet skirt. She trembled with the tension of maintaining her composure on what had seemed the longest ride of her life. Without a word to Lord Wakefield or the groom, she hastened inside as fast as she could without falling headfirst up the steps. His kiss had caught her unaware, the cad. Not a word of censure had come to mind, nor a word of cleverness either.

She had simply leaned into his embrace, drawn to the sweet softness of his lips, feeling a tingly sensation to the tips of her toes. Surprise quickly turned to delight, almost instantly to disgust. But she issued no gasp of horror, no cry of protest, no slap of condemnation. And no real apology came from him either.

She tore up the first flight of stairs and paused to catch her breath. The tapestry on the landing was one of her favorites in the entire house, a sylvan scene of the goddess Diana in her bath. Now, for the first time, she noticed the edge of the work. Acteon, caught in the act of admiring Diana, was turning into a stag.

Angrily she flung herself up the remaining stairs. Why couldn't she have the talents of the chaste Diana?

To make Lord Wakefield a stag and unloose his own dogs to tear him to shreds sounded like an ideal plan.

Her room was empty, and she crumpled to the dressing table bench, letting the sketchbook drop to the floor. The kiss, momentarily so gentle and delicious, meant only one thing. Lord Wakefield thought of her as less than a servant, a toy for his amusement. She'd heard a story once of how a maid in some duke's household was expected to accept the advances of her master. The very thought made her shudder. If that was how Lord High-and-Haughty was going to treat her, she ought to leave Wakefield Hall at once.

Meg pulled off her half-boots and stepped out of the skirt, leaving it in a heap on the floor. A glance in the mirror made her cheeks flame. She looked so very different. Was that what a kiss brought on? Or was the brightness of her eyes due to the tears she should have shed? Was the tilt of the little hat pinned into her curls responsible for the knowing look she wore? Or was she now forever changed by that kiss from a simple country miss to a handsome lady, fashionable and impure?

Could one kiss cause such a change? It was her first kiss, after all.

Shuddering with the enormity of her unanswerable questions, she pulled the pins from her hair and took off the hat, combing her fingers through her curls. No matter how she tried, she couldn't recapture the Meg she knew.

A scratching at the door startled her out of her reverie. "Come."

She could not remember the name of the maid who entered. "Her ladyship and Miss Olivia are in the salon taking tea with some callers, miss. They ask that you join them."

"Oh, I am sorry, I cannot. Please thank them for their kindness, but I am much too dirty to come down."

"Can I send up a bath for you, miss?"

"Please do. I would be most appreciative."

The girl nodded, dipped a curtsy, and left. Meg shrugged her shoulders. At least someone considered her worthy of respect.

Meg took off the jacket and placed it neatly on the bed. Certainly that servant girl was too plain to attract Lord High-and-Haughty, was she not? Or did she have to endure his unwanted touching? Or even warm his bed? Or might she go to him eagerly? A sudden pang of jealousy churned inside her.

Again, Meg's cheeks burned with embarrassment and rage. How could she think such things? She clasped her arms around herself to quell another shiver. In so doing she caught a glimpse of herself in the tall cheval glass in the corner. Clad only in a white shift, she looked quite small and thin, almost scrawny. Lord High-and-Haughty's kiss must have been nothing but a sham, a way of establishing his control, his hegemony, over her.

Well, she was not going to be his plaything to kiss whenever the fancy took him. No indeed, she would tell him outright she wanted no more of his company. When she rode back to the lake, Benjamin was all the company she needed.

Nor was the earl going to drive her away. She was far too eager to earn the countess's fee for her painting. Let him think the money was all she cared about.

Why, she could even threaten to tell Lady Wakefield

what a churl her grandson was, taking advantage of a poor but respectable young lady like herself. Let the countess reprimand her wayward grandson.

But that didn't seem very probable. Lady Wakefield adored her Nicky, whether he deserved it or not.

She would have to tell him herself not to trifle with her. That was the only way. And she had the rest of the afternoon, soaking in a bath, to draw up the right words.

When he heard his grandmother requested his presence in the salon, Nicholas bit back a curse. He had seen the carriage waiting in the stable yard when he returned the horses to Jed's care. The very last thing he wanted was to rush out of his riding clothes in order to attend the countess and her callers.

But he knew how much it meant to his grandmama to have him back at Wakefield Hall, and of course he knew part of her pleasure was to show him off to her visitors. Since he planned to leave again in the morning, he hurried Eason to rid himself of the britches soiled from sitting on the damp ground and finish his toilet with a minimum of fuss.

Entering the salon, he almost cringed to see Mrs. Evans, the vicar's wife, and Lady Duckworth taking tea with Lady Wakefield and Miss Olivia.

"Ah, here he is." The countess's face bore more than her usual tinge of mischievousness as she greeted him.

Nick bowed to the guests and Miss Olivia before he went to his grandmama and touched his lips to the gnarled hand she offered him.

"Take a seat, Nicholas, and satisfy the curiosity of

the ladies who spotted you tooling through the village
yesterday."

"Oh my, no, my lord," snuffled Mrs. Evans. "Not
curiosity, oh, no. Nothing so vulgar as that. We were
just so surprised to see you back in Berkshire."

Nicholas wondered how many of the village women
had been in the delegation that sent Mrs. Evans and
Lady Duckworth to ferret out the information. It was
a wonder they hadn't managed to ambush him on the
way back home from Wallingford. Nosy old cats.

"Lady Wakefield has been telling us about her conservatory project." Lady Duckworth's shrill voice
grated on his senses.

"And how you found the perfect artist to complete
its decor."

If Lady Duckworth was strident, Mrs. Evans was a
gushing stream of chatter.

She went on. "And I told your grandmama, I said,
how very fine it is of you to bring Miss Olivia along.
She says they are on the third chapter of *Waverley,*
which I truly admire because I have never enough time
to read . . ."

He tuned out, turning his gaze to Miss Olivia, who
was trying to stifle a smile. She wouldn't be smiling
long, not after she talked to her sister and learned of
his confounded, unexplainable breach of good manners
earlier that afternoon.

Breach of good manners, hell! He had succumbed
to the basest kind of instinct, kissing that cunning little
wench purely on a whim of the moment. *Ah, Wakefield,
you cork-brained nodcock!*

He realized that Miss Olivia was now looking at
him with a questioning gaze, no doubt wondering why
he seemed to be staring at her. He gave her a little

half-smile and a nod of his head, both of which she returned. If he did not know better, he would judge his behavior to be that of a green stripling, completely unfamiliar with acceptable drawing-room manners, instead of the gentleman he liked to think he was. Always a man of perfectly correct behavior in the presence of ladies, a pattern card of respectability, a man never ruled by caprice, never guided by emotion. Except, that is, where his grandmama was concerned.

"Nicholas, I have not explained to the ladies how you met Miss Hayward. I am sure they would enjoy the story."

Oh, indeed, they would enjoy the story, but he was not about to tell it. "We met in London, almost by chance. As I recall, Miss Hayward was engaged in the admiration of some statuary, is that not correct, Miss Olivia?"

Her sharp intake of breath was nearly a gasp, but she recovered quickly. "Why, yes, an Apollo I believe."

To his utter amazement, Nicholas felt a warm flush suffuse his face as he thought of Miss Hayward studying the statue's naked loins. He stole another glance at Miss Olivia, whose cheeks were also stained with a rosy glow.

"How very interesting." Mrs. Evans leaned forward, silently urging him to continue the story.

"It was a fortunate coincidence." Nicholas would not add another word to the story, neither one iota of the truth nor the slightest falsehood.

"Nicholas, your reticence amazes me." The countess spoke in a voice as sweet as honey and suitably sticky with sarcasm.

He gave her his most innocent grin. "I know how

little you care for current London goings-on, Grandmama. How often I have heard you say what skimbleskamble nonsense passes for polite society these days."

He was rewarded by her quick burst of laughter.

Mrs. Evans dove into the breach. "The things one hears are enough to curdle the cream. Prince George is not a credit to his father in the way he cavorts with all sorts of rabble, gambling I hear, until his debts . . ."

As Mrs. Evans's words tumbled on and on, Nicholas tried to preserve his mask of innocent indifference. Miss Olivia still stared at him, no doubt wondering about his version of their meeting. Lady Duckworth's beady eyes over her tightly pursed lips seemed riveted to him. And his grandmama's slyly quizzical gaze focused on him too. *Mrs. Evans, I bow to your silvery tongue.*

He hardly moved a muscle as his grandmama's guest catalogued the latest *on-dits* to make their way from town to their little corner of Berkshire. Just when he thought she would never stop, Mrs. Evans began to exclaim about overstaying her welcome. That, he knew from past experience, preceded her departure by about ten more minutes, ten minutes that would be devoted to her most gracious thanks, compliments to the countess, to cook for the excellent cake, to the taste of the household that sought out such rare blends of tea, and final comments upon the vagaries of the weather, which was bound to change any moment to exactly the kind of winds that would bring the vicar, her husband, a dreadful catarrh. . . .

When at last the humdrum recital was finished, Nicholas escorted Mrs. Evans and Lady Duckworth, whose reserve he so thankfully appreciated, to their carriage and assisted them into their seats. He hoped his gallantry would make a more lasting impression than the paucity of details he had given about his meeting with Miss Hayward.

As he waved good-bye, he supposed he ought to be grateful Miss Hayward had not made an appearance in the salon. All the way back to the house from the lake, he had felt her silent condemnation like an unreachable burr in his boot. It was easier to put up with its sting for a short time than to stop and try to correct matters without, in one case, a ready explanation, and in the other, a bootjack.

He made a detour into the library before going back to the countess. If there had been anything stronger and more satisfying than sherry within his reach, he would have finished off the whole bottle.

When he went back into the salon, Miss Olivia was reading again from a red-bound volume he quickly recognized as Scott. She had a soft but animated voice, one that would help lull Grandmama into complete reliance upon the sisters. God only knew what would go on here in his absence.

"Excuse me, Grandmama, Miss Olivia." He kept his innocent expression in place.

"Yes, Nicky, you rascal. You fobbed off Mrs. Evans and Lady Duckworth quite disgracefully."

"You know how I abhor being the object of their gossip."

"My boy, as I have told you over and over again, gossip is the glue that sticks this village together. Of what use would we quality folk be if we did not provide the subject matter for the rest of them. I declare there is certainly no other use for any queen or king or prince or duke I have ever known. Every scrap of information, every detail of your address, every nuance of your tone, my dear, will feed the fire of their chatter."

Nicholas nodded. "As always, Grandmama, you see the truth of it. I concede the point."

"There is no need to be sarcastic, Nicholas."

"I beg your pardon. I did not intend to cause offense."

"You certainly have not offended me. But a cynical view is not appealing, you know."

"Might I bring you a glass of sherry?"

"Since I have no doubt you wish to have another, I shall join you. Miss Olivia?"

The younger Miss Hayward, whom he'd noted from the corner of his eye as an avid follower of the barbed exchange, shook her head. "No, thank you. I am not accustomed—"

The countess waved her hand. "Perhaps you should go up to your sister, my dear. See that she is not overtired."

Livy dipped a curtsy. "Thank you, Lady Wakefield."

The countess watched Livy limp across the room and close the door behind her. "A pity nothing can be done about her foot. She is a charming child."

Nicholas groaned inwardly. Just as he had feared, the sisters were indeed skewering their way into his grandmama's confidence. It was abominable how gullible she was. He could be gone only a short time and he would have to be on guard to be sure she was not gulled out of some valuable possessions. It made him angry to think of the little tarts imposing on her good nature. The situation was becoming more and more intolerable by the moment.

Nicholas sat near his grandmother, taking her tiny, fragile hand in his. "I must beg you to excuse me from dinner tonight. I have some business for which I must return to London in the morning, and before I go, I want to talk over a few matters with Stevenson. We will take dinner at the inn."

"Hummpf, more kindling for fires of gossip. What is the earl doing in conference with his bailiff?"

Nicholas laughed. "I consider such speculation entirely harmless. And, as you have so recently pointed out, part of my duty to the neighborhood."

"You are leaving early?"

"Yes, probably at first light. The sooner I get to town, the sooner I can finish up and return."

"Meg, where have you been?" Livy burst through the door and went to the little desk where Meg was doodling on her drawing pad.

"Right here, in our room." Meg picked up a separate sheet. "What do you think of this?"

Livy did not take the sketch. "Lady Wakefield had callers, and she expected you to come down. Why would you stay up here alone?"

Meg was eager to tell Livy all about this morning, especially the earl's affronts to her modesty. But looking into her sister's unusually animated face, Meg changed her mind."I am . . . fatigued after riding across the estate."

"You? Done in by a little exercise? But never mind. I must tell you all about the ladies who called. One was a hook-nosed old crone called Lady Duckworth, who stared down her nose, and the other was Mrs.

Evans, the vicar's wife, who talks ceaselessly. They came to find out about you. About us."

Meg wrinkled her nose. "About us?"

Livy rushed on. "Villagers saw Lord Wakefield and you driving to town yesterday."

"Everyone's imaginations went wild, I suppose."

"The countess told the earl his only reason for being was to satisfy the need of the villagers for gossip!"

Meg sighed. What would the old biddies think if they knew what he had done this morning? "Whatever did he say?"

"He agreed, though he said he despised tittle-tattle."

"I am not surprised." Meg listened as Livy went on to describe the two visitors and what they said. "Then the countess asked the earl to explain how he met you."

"Oh, dear, how did he answer?" Meg's voice sounded shaky even to herself.

Livy was too involved in her story to notice. "Oh, Meg, he said he met you admiring some statuary. Like it was at an exhibition of sculpture or something." She burst into laughter.

"I was aghast, afraid he would tell what part of that Apollo's body we were studying."

Meg felt suddenly short of breath, and her whisper was hardly more than a croak. "I had forgotten . . . I had forgotten."

While her sister chattered on, Meg wished she could simply disappear from Wakefield Hall and never see the earl again. How had she forgotten the Apollo on his staircase, forgotten the earl overheard her talking about its intimate parts? *So that is what he thinks of me. A hussy with entirely indecent thoughts. No wonder he trifled with me.*

Her sketch for one of the walls lay abandoned on the desk. Her mind spun in entirely new—and unwelcome—directions. Convincing the Earl of Wakefield she was an innocent was impossible. How could she prove herself pure and unsullied if she did not bring up the very subject that was improper to discuss? Exactly the same situation as trying to prove she was not a swindler. No claims of virtue would suffice. How could she redeem a reputation she never had?

Could she just tell him she was a country girl with no experience? Of course he already knew that, but instead of blamelessness he probably suspected country people were full of cunning and malevolence, at the very least gossipers who thrived on rumors of scandal.

Meg hardly moved as Livy changed into her better gown, a tired muslin. The new ribbon trim only made it look shabbier. Meg felt close to tears. The task she had begun in order to rectify an honest mistake had turned into a disaster. And no matter how much she resented the earl's boldness, she hoped that someday he would kiss her again. Which only proved she wasn't as innocent as she wished to be.

As on the previous days, they joined the countess in her drawing room before dinner.

Lady Wakefield asked Livy for another chapter of *Waverley* before they went to the table. Livy took the book from a footman and began to read.

"Chapter Five, in which . . ."

Livy read, and Meg fidgeted as she waited for the earl's arrival. Her stomach fluttered like a hummingbird's wing. How could she force down a single morsel of food?

She fixed her gaze on the Gainsborough portrait of the countess and her husband. She could visualize them walking across the bridge she had sketched that morning. They would sit on the grass, or perhaps a stone bench to admire the view, their own lake on their lovely estate. And the earl might lean over to his wife, tip up her chin with his thumb, and press a kiss on her soft lips. Meg squeezed her eyes shut and tried to curb the memory of that morning's kiss from another earl.

Stop that immediately, she told herself. She forced herself to look again at the portrait. Someplace on the conservatory walls, she would paint the countess and her earl into the scene.

But however she tried to concentrate on the job ahead, she could not quell the pounding heartbeat, the damp palms that betrayed her jangled nerves. Nicholas, Lord Wakefield, would come into the room any moment now.

She had not yet bested the earl in conversation despite the many times she had carefully prepared a setdown to deliver. Now she had not a thing ready to say, not even a faint idea of how she might proceed. And when he appeared, at any moment, he would be all that was elegant and proper on the surface. Down deep he would be thinking what a hoyden she was, wondering what prurient thoughts must be stirring in her head, even considering how she intended to swindle his grandmother. And she would look all a muddle in her worn gown and ink-stained fingers.

Whatever could she say to reverse his distorted view of her? No one she had ever known had thought her either a criminal or guilty of impure thoughts. She was quite accustomed to being considered dutiful and virtuous, anything but a jade, a wayward woman of loose morals. How could she prove she was not what she had never been?

Livy stopped reading and closed the book as the butler entered. He bowed to the countess and offered her his arm. Livy took her other elbow and Meg was left to follow them into the dining room.

So Lord High-and-Haughty would make a ceremonial grand entrance, she supposed. He would beg their pardon for his deplorable tardiness and then, inevitably, she would have to meet his eyes. They would shine with a sardonic glint that only she would see, spearing her with his knowledge that this afternoon she had kissed him with the wantonness of a fast woman.

She closed her eyes with the pain of the thought and half tripped. An arm caught hers, but when she opened her eyes, it was only a footman, waiting to seat her at the table.

"Thank you," she murmured, sliding into the chair he held.

The countess, once settled, sighed deeply. "But for you gels, I would be alone again this evening. Nicholas is taking dinner with Mr. Stevenson to discuss some estate matters, and he is leaving in the morning for a few days."

Meg clasped her napkin to her mouth to stifle a chirp of surprise and relief.

The countess did not notice, nodding to the butler to place a small cutlet on her plate. "Nicholas is so very much like my late husband, the eighth earl, very conscientious and purposeful. Strange how his father was so different."

Meg felt as though a great stone had been lifted off

her chest and she could breath deeply once more. With a hand that trembled only slightly, she raised her goblet and took a sip of wine. How fortunate he would be away for a few days. Perhaps his poor estimation of her would have faded by the time he returned. Or perhaps, if she hurried and his trip was of an extended length, she might be nearly finished painting.

Lady Wakefield seemed in a talkative mood. "Richard, my son and Nicky's father, devoted himself to racing his horses. He had a fine stable here at the Hall, but I am afraid he wagered rather more than he could afford. When he won, he used his prize to buy more horses, but when he lost, he never sold. Richard was a rare judge of horseflesh, but it led him astray. The Old Earl, my husband, was never one to gamble. I was certain our son would follow his father's example, but alas, Richard cared more for winning horse races than anything else in the world. More than caring for Wakefield Hall. The stables were always the finest, but . . ." Her voice, sad, trailed away.

"The earl, your grandson, seems to love horses too." Livy smiled at the countess. "He rides a handsome gray."

"Ah, yes. Nicholas is a fair judge of equine excellence. But he has sold off most of the racing stock. If you look closely, my dear, even from the windows of the house, you will see the horses in the fields are heavy-bred, suitable for farm work. Beautiful, I suppose, in their own right, but not the sort that gentlemen choose to ride and race."

Meg listened carefully, turning over in her mind the new information on the earl. When he had come back to Wakefield to take on his title and the responsibilities of his estate, he must have been disappointed in what he found. Perhaps there had been debts to settle, debts that caused him to sell the horses his father loved. That would have been difficult for any son.

Hah! Here she was feeling pity for the man. If she lived for a thousand years, she would never be able to sort out her inconsistent feelings about the tenth Earl of Wakefield.

Seven

Nicholas sipped his claret as he listened to the talk swirl around the table at White's. He was not fond of the London club, preferring the quiet of his own library. But he was looking for information and he would most likely find it there.

"What of Jonathan Fenton?" he asked at a break in the discussion of the news from Vienna. "Is he in town?"

Sir Perry Sotherton shook his head. "My man tells me his mother insisted he continue his recuperation at home at Waylands. Poor lad, without his right arm."

"And what of Gunderson?" someone asked.

"Another case of exhaustion, they say . . ."

Nicholas let his attention stray from the conversation. So many of his fellow army officers, his former fellows, that is, had lost more than limbs on the fields of Belgium. The battle, he heard, had been short, intense, and bloody with the French fighting savagely for their former emperor, that despicable Corsican now, at last, dispatched to the very edge of the earth, a place too good for him. Nicholas fought off the waves of regret that assailed him whenever the wars were talked of. He had spent nearly all the years of his youth serving the crown, but never within the sound of gunfire. His had been a career spent in or-

ganizing home defenses, tasks of little personal satisfaction and no glory whatsoever. With what satisfaction could he boast of building a dozen Martello
Towers, of drilling rank upon rank of country militia
armed with scythes and rakes instead of rifles or even
worn-out muskets? How he had chafed at the indignity
of it all, but he had done his duty as ordered, keeping
his complaints to himself. Except when he had shared
them with Jonathan, so long condemned to the same
sort of service.

But later, after his father died and Nicholas was called
home to assume his role as head of a long-established
noble family, Jonathan had achieved his desire, a bat-
tlefield to fight upon in the service of Wellington. How
ironic, how very unmerited had been his friend's fate.
To have fought on until, at the very brink of victory, he
had received a vile blow that cost him his arm and, it
had been rumored, part of his sanity.

Nicholas felt almost guilty about the plan he had
for Jonathan now. Yes, his friend would no doubt recover his health and most of his reason eventually, and
Nicholas hoped to speed up the process by bringing
him to Wakefield. But Nicholas had other motives too.
With Jonathan at hand, Nicholas could spend most of
his time away from the Hall while keeping close
enough to protect his grandmama from any schemes
Miss Hayward might concoct. Lucky that his two goals
fit together so nicely and were so entirely admirable.

"I say, Wakefield, have you nodded off?" Sir Perry
poked at his arm.

"Sorry. Simply wondering if that Corsican monster
is a good swimmer." Nicholas reached for the claret.
Tomorrow he would go to Kent, collect Jonathan, and
get back to Wakefield Hall without delay. But he had

one more task to accomplish in London, and he had no idea to whom to apply for the repair of a badly torn fan. None of these jolly fellows would have the least idea either . . . unless Sotherton's connection with that comely young actress might suffice.

Nicholas waited for the conversation to reach a boisterous level, then leaned close to Sir Perry.

"Are you still seeing Miss Rich of the Theatre Royal?" he whispered.

Sotherton slapped his shoulder. "See her? Great ghosts, Wakefield, she costs me more than my stable of prime goers! In a few minutes I must collect her from the greenroom after tonight's performance."

"Might I accompany you backstage? I have a little commission for a handy theatrical props man."

"Just so you don't trespass on my territory, my friend."

"No, indeed." He gave a teasing chuckle. "Not tonight anyway. I am leaving town again early in the morning."

"You dog! Never known you to have a taste for lightskirts before." Perry gave him another cuff, then turned back to the group.

Nicholas gazed through the ruby lens of his wine. Perry was correct. For many years Nicholas had successfully shielded himself from entangling affairs. And yearnings for females rarely disturbed his wits. Until now.

So what was going on in his head? He was usually not a man who suffered from self-delusion. So why was he glossing over a prime reason for wanting Jonathan on hand? His inexplicable attraction to that little vixen was impossible to deny. With Jonathan at

Wakefield, he could insulate himself from the infernal enticements of Miss Meg Hayward.

The next day, as Livy read to Lady Wakefield and Meg sketched, Sutton arrived in the conservatory with an attractive woman who looked to Meg's eye to be nearing forty, perhaps less if her countenance had not been spoiled by a stiff glower. She wore a handsome gown of deep green trimmed with scallops of rose velvet. Her head of curly dark hair resembled the earl's, set off with a small hat sporting several pink feathers.

"Lady Ella Birmingham," Sutton announced.

"My dearest Grandmama!" Lady Ella kissed both of the countess's cheeks.

"Pray allow me to introduce you to my guests, Miss Hayward, and Miss Olivia Hayward. This is Nicholas's sister, Ella Birmingham."

As she tried to execute a curtsy while holding her sketchpad, Meg felt Lady Ella's intense stare drilling right through her. Olivia stood and gave her crooked bow, and for a moment Lady Ella's glare turned to her.

"I am pleased to make your acquaintance, Lady Ella," Meg said.

"As am I," Livy added.

Lady Ella looked back and forth between Meg and her sister. "Grandmama, I must speak with you in private."

Meg prepared to set down her pad and charcoal. She suspected Lady Ella had caught a whiff of gossip, though the urgency of her manner seemed excessive.

"My dear Ella," the countess said. "You have said nothing about my conservatory. Is this not the first

time you have seen it all finished? Except for the painting and the greenery, that is."

"Yes, quite lovely. Very nice indeed." Lady Ella's
sour gaze turned back to Meg, then to Livy.

Meg saw Livy mark her place and close the novel.

"There is no need for you to leave, gels."

"But, Grandmama . . ."

"No fussing, Ella. I know why you have arrived all
atwitter. Put your mind at ease. Sutton, please bring
us refreshments."

When he was gone, the countess spoke again. "I am
not one for roundaboutation. You have no doubt received a number of reports about Nicholas. He has
been seen accompanying a young lady about the countryside, is that not right? Or have you heard some juicy
on-dits from London? If so, I insist you share them
with me."

"Why, Grandmama, how you talk."

"Give over, Ella. Or are you having more contretemps with your rascal of a son? Jason seems to delight
in being as naughty as his father was."

"Lord Birmingham never misbehaved."

"So that is what he told you!"

Lady Ella's cheeks flamed.

"Now, now, Ella, I am teasing."

"Oh, Grandmama, you know just how to put me in
a state."

The countess paused while Sutton set the tray in
front of her. "Please do the honors, Ella. How are the
little ones?"

As she filled the teacups, Lady Ella expounded
upon the health of her youngest children, all apparently
robust.

Meg's fingers itched to pick up her pad and charcoal

again. She longed to do a sketch of the earl's sister, who resembled him so closely. Instead, she took the offered teacup and sat as quietly as Livy.

The countess resumed her questioning. "Where is Jason these days?"

Lady Ella sighed. "The boy is off with some friends in Norfolk, though what they are doing I dare not ask. Birmingham has refused to send him a penny more before his next quarterly allowance. If he has been pestering Nicholas, I shall be very angry with him."

"Jason or Nicky?"

"Jason, unless Nicholas was foolish enough to give him any money. Then I shall be quite put out with him too."

"No matter how I provoke you, Ella, know that I understand completely what you must endure. Your father was a wild young man, as you well know. Which is not to say that your husband necessarily behaved like an angel."

"I am sure he did not. But I never heard of him . . . enough of that. You were correct. I came because I heard gossip concerning Nicholas."

"These things simply fly around the county on the wings of the birds?"

"As you said, he has been seen with a young woman, and it is said he will marry her this summer."

Meg nearly gasped out loud. Certainly that young woman could not be her, could it? As soon as the notion leaped into her mind, she knew it could not be so. Never would his high-and-haughtiness think of wedding the likes of her.

The countess gave a gleeful bark of laughter. "My, how the story has grown. The tabbies arrived the moment he drove through the village taking Miss Hayward to Wallingford for some supplies. And now it has ballooned into a proposal. How very amusing."

"I did not find it amusing when two of my friends wanted more information. I said I had not heard anything."

Meg did not find it amusing either; she bit down on her tongue to keep from saying something out loud. Lady Ella again turned her pinched scrutiny in Meg's direction.

The countess waved her hand at Meg. "Is that so, my dear? Has Nicky made you an offer?"

"No, my lady. In fact, I believe the earl would rather he had never met me. Though he has been all that is proper," she added quickly if untruthfully.

"There you have it, Ella. You cannot confirm with Nicky because he has gone off on some duty or other for the next few days. Now that I have the Misses Hayward here to entertain me, I hardly miss him."

For the first time, Lady Ella smiled. "I am gratified to hear it. So you are just a painter here to do Grandmama's walls?"

"Yes." Meg wondered why Lady Ella's correct designation of her role sounded so demeaning. What should she care what Lady Ella thought of her? Except that she was the earl's sister . . .

Lady Ella cast her narrowed eyes on Livy. "And you are just her sister?"

"Yes, my lady." Livy's tone almost offered a challenge, Meg thought.

The countess shook her head. "The gels are here as my guests, Ella. Now, I will give you something a little different to feed the gabblemongers. Next month I will hold a ball for Nicholas's birthday."

A ball? Here at Wakefield Hall?

"Oh, my little brother will be thirty, will he not? I had forgotten that important event. May I send someone over to assist you with the invitations?"

"No, dear. I am sure the Misses Hayward will assist."

Livy answered quickly. "I would be honored to help while Meg paints."

"You see? They are excellent companions in all regards."

"Then I must hurry home," Lady Ella said, casting one more quelling look at Meg.

Meg bit her tongue as Lady Ella made her proper farewells. She had the same arrogance as her brother, and not even when she spoke of her children had her countenance softened appreciably.

The countess rang the little bell beside her and again Sutton's footsteps sounded across the tile.

After Lady Ella had left, the countess chuckled to herself. "Ah, she is off to spread the news as fast as she can. Miss Hayward, what did you think of my eldest granddaughter?"

"She seemed all that was gracious and proper." Meg decided she had become a rather accomplished liar.

"Humbug. Like all my children and grandchildren, even my great-grandchildren, she seems to have a difficult time finding a balance in her life. All of them are either loose screws or as pedantic and stiff-rumped as an old vicar. In my day we knew how to have a good time without tipping the world askew, but these days, I do not understand what makes some of them so niffy-naffy and some so staid and starchy. Miss Olivia, can we resume our chapter?"

As Livy reached for the book, Meg slowly unclenched her hands and wiggled her fingers to loosen them. *What would you think, Lady Wakefield, if I told you that your staid and starchy Nicholas kissed me yesterday at the lake?*

Nicholas barely suppressed a gasp of shock when he saw Jonathan. His formerly strong and fit friend huddled in a chair, heavy shawl around his shoulders and face so thin and haggard he seemed almost a corpse. Only his shock of reddish-brown hair proved that the wraith was truly Captain Jonathan Fenton.

"Jon, how are you getting along?" Nick's question was entirely spurious. Clearly, his health was terrible, his mood worse.

"What are you doing here?" Jonathan's voice was weak but his words were uttered harshly.

"Came to find you. I need you at Wakefield Hall."

The sound Jonathan uttered was neither a malicious laugh nor a pathetic sob but something in between.

Without waiting for an invitation, Nicholas pulled a chair near Jonathan's and sat beside him. "Come, old friend, are you suffering a great deal of pain?"

Lady Fenton bustled into the room, her hands full of bowls and flannels. "What is this? Nicholas, I mean, Lord Wakefield, when did you arrive. Whatever is the matter, my darling boy . . . oh, are you deviling him, my lord? Wherever is Chalmers?"

Nicholas stood and bowed, took one bowl, apparently of gruel, from Lady Fenton's hands. "Madam, I have just arrived, and I assure you I have only Jonathan's best interests in mind."

She spoke as if her son could not hear. "Oh, he is so weak, Nicholas, so woefully frail. We do all we can to help, but he is sadly slipping instead of improving."

Nicholas watched Jonathan's face and saw no change in his tortured expression.

Lady Fenton turned her attention to another female, a maid, who entered. "Polly, bring the laudanum immediately. Hurry."

Nicholas frowned. "Is this what the doctor recommends?"

Abruptly Jonathan straightened up. "Get out, all of you. Leave me alone. But send in the draft."

"I shall return shortly, Jonathan. I am serious about my need for you." Without waiting for a response, Nicholas picked up the gruel and followed the now-weeping mother out of the room.

"My dear Lady Fenton, let us sit down and discuss Jonathan's condition, well out of his earshot."

She pressed a handkerchief to her wet cheeks and led him to a nearby parlor, where she broke down completely.

Nicholas listened for the better part of an hour to her heartrending and gloomy recital, from Jonathan's arrival at Waylands through his steady deterioration. Interspersed with many tears, she told how Jonathan refused to talk about his wounds, how he could not bring himself to accept the loss of his right arm or to follow the orders of any of the several doctors and apothecaries they had summoned to his side.

"I fear he is in terrible pain, and even the laudanum gives little relief. He hardly eats. He stays in the dark but refuses to sleep. His sisters come and go, but he does not wish to see them, or, indeed, anyone."

Nicholas patted the hand of the distraught matron. "I can see you have done everything you could for him. If I might try to help, my lady, I cannot promise success, but I have heard of other cases like his. I cannot pretend to do more in treating his physical ills, but the cause of his decline might be due to more than his wounds."

"Oh, say you do not mean brain fever or delirium."

"Nothing permanent, but the effects of his battle experience and the debilitating loss of his arm. I propose taking Jonathan with me to Wakefield Hall. Perhaps a change of scene will help his temperament. I assure you he will receive the best of care."

She began to weep anew. "How can I let him go when he is so weak? If only his father were still with us . . ."

"Lady Fenton, you are sadly worn down. You need your rest, to restore yourself in order to help Jonathan. If your health fails, you will not be able to nurse your son. I can take him to Berkshire for a few weeks, while you rest and return to your full powers."

"I so wish I could help him, bring him back to his sunny self. But I am failing."

"Remembrance of your devotion, and his father's, will always be with him. At Wakefield, our excellent doctor, who attends my grandmama nearly every day, will be on hand."

Lady Fenton rose and walked to a window.

Nicholas continued. "I shall write to you every week, and if he does not improve by the end of the summer, I will bring him back to Waylands."

He went to stand beside her. "I have dealt with many men from my militia who returned from the Peninsula and suffered greatly but were able to recover and find a purpose to their lives. There is every hope that Jonathan can do the same."

At last she nodded. "He has always admired you,

Nicholas. I believe that if anyone can help my son, you are the man."

Later that night, as he lay in an unfamiliar bedchamber at Waylands, Nick hoped with all his being his pledge to Lady Fenton would not be in vain.

Meg felt a shiver of nerves as she entered the conservatory. The sun was not strong, hiding behind a film of thin clouds. This was the day she both dreaded and craved, the day she would begin her actual work. For more than a week, she had put off this moment, delaying unconscionably, until she ran out of excuses to herself.

She chose one of the five flat pilasters for her first attempt and ran her fingers over its surface, almost praying she would find a flaw severe enough to postpone the commencement of the painting. The texture was perfect.

Meg sighed and lifted her charcoal to make the first mark. Her table was in place with the sketch she intended to replicate and all her supplies laid out in a convenient arrangement. Yet to draw a line meant a kind of assurance she certainly did not feel inside.

How had she gotten herself into such a muddle? She was entirely unqualified for this job, as the earl had pointed out that first morning. If he could see her now, standing there trembling, would he not laugh? But if he had been in the room, or even within shouting distance, she would never have allowed herself to shake or exhibit the tiniest confirmation of her hesitation. His exasperation acted as her strongest stimulus to accepting the project, probably stronger even than the money her family needed so badly.

She drew a deep breath and pulled the charcoal in a curve across and downward, defining the swag of roses that would wind about the Grecian-style column she intended to depict. If her skill was up to it, she wanted each of the pilasters to give the effect of a rounded column draped with rose-covered boughs. From a distance, no one would be able to tell the pilasters were completely flat.

Once she began, the next lines were easier and easier. When the countess and Livy appeared a half hour later, she had almost all of the sketching finished.

"Miss Hayward, you must have arisen very early. Do you wish a cup of chocolate? Some biscuits?" Sutton helped the countess from her Bath chair to the chaise and propped the pillows behind her.

Meg realized she was terribly hungry when she turned to dip a curtsy to Lady Wakefield. "Yes, my lady, that would be appreciated."

"Sutton, if you please?"

The butler, ever solicitous, bowed and nodded.

Livy took a chair next to the sofa. "Meggy, you have finished your outline."

"Not quite, but nearly so. What do you think?"

The countess squinted across the room. "To my old eyes, it looks like . . . ah, it don't look like much of anything. Tell me how the colors will go."

Meg grinned because the more she looked at the markings, the more she realized her work began creditably, despite Lady Wakefield's remark. "These straight lines show the column's dimensions and the curves show the roses winding around."

"Ah! Now I see. Just like that little painting you did last Sunday?"

"Yes, exactly."

"But, Miss Hayward, you are wearing your gown without a bit of protection. Are you not afraid you will soon be wearing a layer of charcoal dust? Or that you will spatter paint on it?"

"I have nothing else. Perhaps I should ask someone in the kitchen for an apron."

"I have a better idea."

Sutton brought the tray of chocolate and a basket of rolls. The countess whispered in his ear and the butler hurried away again. Before Meg had finished her chocolate and a sweet bun, he came back carrying what seemed to be one of the earl's white shirts.

"This should be sufficient to cover your gown." The countess took the shirt from Sutton, held it up, and cocked her head to one side. "Nicky will never miss it. Here, my dear."

Meg walked slowly over to the chaise and grasped the shirt by the neck, trying to beat back the waves of discomfiture that brought warmth to her cheeks.

"Put it on. See if it will do."

The fabric felt soft and supple, a fine lawn as smooth as silk. When she slipped her arms into the sleeves, she felt almost as though the earl touched her and sent her blood racing. "I think it is rather too large." She started to take it off.

"Then that's exactly what you need. You can roll up the cuffs. The farther the hem hangs down, the more protection."

"But what will Lord Wakefield say when he sees I have appropriated one of his shirts?"

"If I know my grandson, he has dozens. You can blame everything on me anyway. Now, go ahead and put it on."

Meg followed her directions, buttoning the shirt and

carefully rolling up the sleeves. She suppressed a little shiver of delight at the softness of her new apparel. The shirt reached nearly to her knees, enfolding the muslin of her skirt.

"Will it do?"

"Yes, Lady Wakefield, thank you very much. It will do just fine, but I fear it may be ruined by my paints."

"Think nothing of it. Better one of Nicky's old shirts than your gown."

Meg nodded. However, she mused, this one shirt was probably worth more than every gown she owned and her shoes combined. And how would she ever be comfortable in a garment that had once encased Lord Wakefield's handsome broad shoulders?

Eight

Nicholas estimated they had covered about half of the distance to Wakefield when Jonathan awoke from a restless sleep."How are you feeling, Jon?"

The answer was little more than a grunt. Jonathan's sunken eyes remained half open.

"Your mother needs a rest."

No response.

"She is beside herself with worry."

At last, Jon stirred. "She should let me die. All I want is to be left alone."

"Why?" Nicholas leaned forward on the seat and put his face close to Jon's. "Why do you want to die?"

"Stubble it, Nick! Get away. You are not helping me. No one is helping, just making things worse."

Nicholas forced himself to give a little laugh. "I'm no angel of mercy, far from it. I have a thoroughly selfish reason for wanting you at Wakefield."

"Ha! You don't have to pretend."

"You'll laugh when you hear what I am doing at the Home Farm. I'm turning my father's championship racing stud into a home for draft horses."

"At least I am not the only demented soul in the realm."

"Demented, but ever practical, Jon. Father's fine racehorses ate enough to feed several entire villages.

But once they were gone, I had empty stalls and a dozen grooms who needed employment. So I have acquired some heavy stock and I need you to help me find more."

"Don't make me laugh." Jon's pallid face shone with sweat, yet he pulled a rug more closely around his shoulders.

"I want to breed for strength, so I need horses like the ones you found to pull the cannons and the supply wagons, good, sturdy—"

"Where are my drops?" Jon clutched at Nick's arm. "Don't try to humor me. Just forget about trying to make me useful."

"I will give you the laudanum only if you agree to help."

"You bastard!" Jon spit out the words and fell shivering back against the cushions.

"You know this stuff is no good for you."

"Just give me the bottle."

Nick held up the vial. "You can see there are only a few drops left. Why not hold out for another hour or so?"

Jon seized the bottle and upended it into his mouth. When he had drained the small amount of liquid, he let it drop to the floor.

"You don't know anything about pain, Nick. Nothing at all." He slumped back and closed his eyes. "Nothing at all."

Nicholas watched Jon's haggard face and uncontrollable trembling. He reached down and picked up the vial, replaced the stopper, and dropped it in his pocket. Before he had left Waylands, he and Lady Fenton carefully prepared half a dozen vials with a drop or two of laudanum each in a few drops of water. He knew

Jon would suffer even more if he was cut off from the drug completely, but a diluted dose might gradually lessen his physical dependence.

His mental state was something else altogether. Whatever Jon needed, Nick was determined to provide, enough to recover every bit of Jon's once-cheerful address.

In the morning room, Meg paged through the folio of engravings of garden scenes, her attention only half on the pictures.

Lord Wakefield had been away from his estate for a week now, the servants whispering he had gone to London. Meg disliked servants' gossip, but she could not eradicate the earl from her thoughts, a most distressing situation. She had to come up with a plan for the smaller of the two conservatory walls, and the necessary concentration simply eluded her.

Livy was in the countess's boudoir, where she and Lady Wakefield retired for the morning after breaking their fast. Meg was sorry to miss the next chapter of the novel, but she needed to find a theme and develop her pattern. With her mind wandering so uncontrollably, she had considerable difficulty sorting out her thoughts. Instead, she turned the leaves, hardly noticing their subject matter, and thought of other things, making a mental list, anything to divert her musings from the absent earl.

First she must finish the painting job and do the best possible work. The five pilasters were almost done, waiting only to dry and have the finishing flourishes applied. The countess was pleased with the progress. Yet the scope of the wall space terrified her.

Yesterday she had managed to sketch most of the design for the larger mural, but she cast off all her previous intentions for the narrower side of the wall. Nothing seemed quite right to blend in with the arcadian lake scene and beech trees.

She had no time to dawdle. She needed to finish and be far away from Wakefield Hall before the earl's birthday ball. Only a few weeks remained before the guests would begin arriving. Among those guests, Livy told her, were a number of young ladies the countess had invited as potential matches for her grandson. Meg hated to think about their sure-to-be impeccable bloodlines, delicate beauty, and fashionable wardrobes. By comparison, in her limp muslin, with the earl's shirt as a smock, she would look a fright.

Which brought her thinking back to Nicholas, Lord Wakefield, and her irresponsible and foolish ruminations on his kiss. At night she dreamed of the gentle touch of his lips, and daydreamed in the morning, afternoon, and evening.

Despite the fact she despised his familiarity with her and questioned his propriety and his motivations, Meg longed for him to kiss her again. She imagined this kiss coming in the sunlight amid the blossoms of the garden, in the moonlight beside the garden wall, in the dimness of the stable, in the midnight inky blackness of the forest, and most scandalously, by a single candlelight in her bedchamber. She lamented her sadly untamed imagination, how defiantly her thoughts recurred, how very audacious were her dreams.

And always skirting the edges of Meg's treacherous thoughts were the most brazen notions of all. She hesitated to give room for them even to enter her head, but sometimes she dreamed of herself as the person who haunted his desires. How very foolish she was. He thought her a thief and a hussy, a swindler and a nobody.

She had no way to prove him wrong. She could only finish the job the countess hired her to do and go home to Sussex to prepare her sisters.

Abruptly she realized she had closed the volume, and she stared at its leather back. She stood and walked around the table and even stamped her foot in exasperation. At this rate, she would not finish her work by Christmas, much less before the birthday ball.

Meg sat herself firmly back into her chair and opened the book of Piranesi plates at the first page. Perhaps she could design a garden among some fanciful ruins, ruins something like the complex and intricate remains of Roman baths and castles before her.

Yesterday, in the middle distance of the largest section of the wall, she had sketched two figures on the old bridge over the lake, representing the countess and her husband. In the background were gentle hillsides and green pastures. A stand of old beeches framed the entire scene, and in the very foreground in the lowest section were the tiny Birdsnest Orchids.

Tomorrow she would climb the scaffolding to begin working on the sky. With a deep sigh, she forced her thoughts again to the other side of the entrance door. The sky would carry over, as would the hillsides and perhaps a distant forest. The rest of the painting could be any combination of complicated ruins such as those she now gazed at, or perhaps simple broken columns twined with ivy or a crumbling statue.

Yes, a statue. And why not the Apollo Belvedere? Just like the one in Lord Wakefield's London residence. A similar copy stood at the end of an avenue of yew hedge in the Wakefield gardens. Why had she not thought of it before? That statue was probably a favorite of Lady Wakefield's.

Inspired, she grabbed her sketchpad and began to draw.

Nicholas came downstairs from watching Jonathan fall asleep in the bailiff's house. "Stevenson, I know I am imposing upon you beyond your duty to oblige."

"Not at all, my lord."

"Oh, I am well aware of the difficulty of the task I've undertaken and how much trouble I am bringing to you. I will spend the night in the trundle next to Captain Fenton, but in the morning, I will have to join my grandmama for a short time. I know she will want a full report on my activities of the last week."

"Indeed she will, my lord. The countess is not one for halfway explanations." Stevenson lit his pipe and blew smoke toward the ceiling of his modest parlor.

Nicholas chuckled, seemingly for the first time in days. "Indeed she is not. Only the most complete accounting will do for her."

"And your plan for the captain?"

"I suspect his lethargy is partially due to too much laudanum. He has taken refuge in the numbness provided by the drug rather than face up to a life without his right arm."

"Ain't as if he is the only man to come home without some of his parts, but I 'magine it's a mighty tough condition to contend with."

"Sadly true. And if he only knew it, Jonathan may be luckier than most. He has family and friends who can provide for him, though I honestly intend to put his expertise to work right here at Wakefield."

Stevenson blew another cloud. "Once he gets over his brain fever, or whatever you call it, he can be a big help."

"I have a supply of laudanum, and when he needs it, we can give him a diluted dose. I already cut back while we traveled."

"You just show me how to fix it and I will follow through."

"Stevenson, I have been thinking. If you come across other amputees from the wars, can you find them a place here?"

"I will do my best, my lord."

"Excellent."

After a night with only a few hours of sleep, Nicholas gave Stevenson a supply of laudanum and set off for his grandmama's interrogation. He found her enjoying a cup of chocolate with the Misses Hayward in the morning room.

"Why, Nicky, you have returned!"

Grandmama's smile warmed his heart as he bowed to the three ladies, stealing a quick glance at Miss Meg Hayward. Her eyes sparkled and she appeared more lovely than he recalled, though clad in her usual faded muslin with her hair twisted behind her head.

"I am indeed back, and I shall require the assistance of all three of you, if you are willing." He kissed Grandmama's cheek and took a seat beside her.

"Willing to do what, Nicholas?" She patted his knee.

"This may not be easy or immediately satisfying, but eventually we will succeed in returning my friend Captain Jonathan Fenton to full health." Nicholas carefully explained, without the more gruesome details, about Jon's problems, both physical and mental, leaving out the particulars about the battle and the drug.

Meg watched the earl as he spoke, looking down only when his eyes turned to her. He never failed to surprise, it seemed. Just when she had assumed he must have some selfish reason for avoiding Wakefield, she was proved entirely incorrect. His purpose had been exactly the opposite, to help a friend in need.

"You have set us an awesome task, Nicholas." The countess looked thoughtful. "But you have the promise of any help I can give. I remember Captain Fenton quite well. You brought him here several times and he had the sunniest of natures. Miss Hayward, Miss Olivia?"

"Why, of course, my lady," Meg said.

"We are accustomed to living with several who are eccentric in varying degrees," Livy added.

"When do you wish to bring him here?" the countess asked.

"In a few days, perhaps, depending upon his progress. He is staying at Stevenson's and I will stay there too."

"Nonsense. You must bring him here to the Hall, where he can be comfortable and well cared for without requiring Stevenson to look after him."

"Now, Grandmama, he does not want company for the time being. And he is just settled in. Until he is better, I could not force him to move again."

"Perhaps. But I shall send over a servant this morning to assist."

"Only with a little food, please. Stevenson has Mrs. James in every day to look after him and she has already enlisted in the battle to return Jon to good spirits."

The countess had a determined thrust to her jaw. "Do not expect me to put up with your arrangements for very long, Nicky. If you cannot bring him here in a few days, I shall have to intervene."

Nicholas laughed out loud, and he noted Meg's attempt to cover her grin. "That is a bargain, Grandmama. That is a bargain."

After nuncheon, Mr. Ames arrived to assist Meg in her first ascent of the scaffolding. Meg was pleased to have his help and complimented him on his work when she realized how easy the structure was to climb.

"Mr. Ames, you are the guiding force of this project. And to think I agreed to it before I even considered all the complications, like canvas and priming and scaffolds."

"My pleasure, Miss Hayward. You and yer sister have done good by the countess, and that makes us all happy. Now I will leave you to yer work, as I wield a paintbrush only when the side of a barn be needin' me."

Meg laughed and waved him on his way. She smoothed her hands down the tails of the earl's shirt. Would he notice what she was wearing if he came into the conservatory today? The thought made her stomach churn, but she was determined to move forward.

She had no more than picked up the paints she had mixed that morning, when Lady Wakefield arrived, pushed in her Bath chair by Sutton and accompanied by Livy.

Once they were settled, without noticing her above them, Meg spoke gently in order not to startle them. "Lady Wakefield, Livy, I am beginning the sky." As she spoke she swept the blue-dipped brush across a section of the wall.

"Why, so you are! I am thrilled to see that part begin." The countess waved and Meg responded with a nod of her head.

"Are you all right up there?" Livy asked.

"It is very sturdy and just like walking on a floor." Meg dipped her brush again and spread the blue sky farther.

"Then I shall have Livy begin reading again. Tell us if you cannot hear."

"I shall indeed." Meg changed brushes and began to outline the dimensions of a fluffy cloud.

Livy's soft voice helped to calm Meg's nerves. The earl probably would not come into the room anyway.

Perhaps a half hour had passed when Meg heard Sutton's voice. "Lady Ella Birmingham, my lady."

"Grandmama! I have some news you will find important." Lady Ella's voice sounded solemn and grave.

Meg peered over her shoulder and saw Livy stand and dip a brief curtsy.

"You remember Miss Olivia, and Miss Hayward is there, overhead."

This time Lady Ella hardly gave her a glance. "May we be alone this time?"

"Is it absolutely necessary?"

Meg watched Livy close the novel and walk from the room. Meg judged how long it would take her to complete the section she worked on. "I can be finished here in five minutes or so, Lady Wakefield."

"No need for you to come down at all, Miss Hayward. Continue your work and pay no mind to us."

"But, Grandmama . . ."

"What is it that brings you here again so soon, Ella? More tittle-tattle? We'll have a tea tray, Sutton, if you please."

Meg kept her face turned away from the two ladies below, but she could not help hearing their every word even though Lady Ella was practically whispering.

"You see, I went to call upon the Duchess of Tetton, who is a cousin of Birmingham's, come to spend the summer at their estate near Pangbourne. It was a long way, but I felt I had to pay her the honor of welcoming her to the neighborhood, if one could call such a distance neighboring."

"And you wanted to hear the news from town, I suppose?"

"Grandmama, I do not wish to bicker with you. But I did wonder about—" She paused as Sutton's footsteps sounded on the tile floor, apparently bringing the tray.

For a few moments Meg heard only the gentle tinkling of silver on china.

At last, Lady Ella resumed her conversation. "The duchess is a woman near my age, I suspect, though she looks much older. The duke was not in residence, expected within the week, she said."

Meg kept as quiet as possible; perhaps the two ladies had forgotten she was even there. She resisted the urge to peek at the countess to see her reaction to the rambling story.

Lady Ella chattered on. "The duchess has several

lovely children, one almost the same age as my dear little Algernon."

At last the countess broke in. "Is that the important news, Ella, or are you merely trying to bore me to flinders?"

"Of course not, Grandmama. You see, I have found a young lady who will make a perfect wife for Nicholas. She is the daughter of the Tettons, a most accomplished young performer on the harp, has perfect address, and is quite appealingly pretty."

Meg listened intently, her brush now still.

"Give me her direction and that of her parents and I will send them a card for the birthday ball."

That dratted ball! Meg had to be finished and far away before this lovely young heiress and who knew how many more eager misses flocked to Wakefield for the occasion.

"She is called Belinda, and she is nearly eighteen years of age. Her mother plans her presentation to the Queen next season. I believe she is ideal material for Nicholas."

"Perhaps so. It is high time he chose himself a countess. Jason will inherit the barony from your husband; he certainly does not need to be the eleventh earl of Wakefield too. I intend to see Nicky's nursery filled before I leave this mortal earth."

"What does my brother say about that?"

"He claims to have his own personal schedule, which he is following to the letter. And I am not allowed to turn up my toes for a good many years, no matter how I feel about it."

"That sounds exactly like him. High-handed as ever."

"Have you spoken to the young lady about him?"

"I have. But I was most discreet. I merely mentioned that my unattached brother, the Earl of Wakefield, also lived in the vicinity. From her smile I believe that pleased Lady Belinda and also caught the attention of her mother."

Meg just bet the earl's proximity caught their attention, all right. Her next slash of blue came out ragged and wobbly.

"I am certain they were pleased to find such an eligible gentleman practically on their doorstep," the countess said, a touch of sarcasm in her tone.

"I have written out their direction for you. When are you planning to send out the cards?"

"We have not begun to write them as yet. But the Misses Hayward and I will consult on the arrangements tomorrow."

Meg had the distinct feeling that they had remembered her presence and were now looking up at the sky she painted.

"Will the conservatory be finished by the festivities?" Lady Ella asked.

"I expect so. We will have a grand opening at the same time. Bring in all the tenants and the villagers—"

"Oh, certainly not, Grandmama. Have them all here in the house?"

"I respect the traditions carried out here for centuries. Our people are often welcome within these walls, as you should remember well from your childhood."

"Birmingham says it makes more sense to keep them outside."

"Bah, Birmingham does not have the ancient roots we have in this family. Nor do the Tettons, as I recall. They are just one of the families distinguished by their toad-eating to those Hanoverians."

"Grandmama, I hope you will not say so when the duke and duchess come for the ball."

"Hmmpf. Some people are far too high in the instep for their own good."

Meg stifled a laugh. Lady Wakefield was giving her granddaughter quite a mouthful to chew.

"I left my carriage at the door, Grandmama, so I'd best be on my way home. I hope you are happy with my discovery."

"We shall see, Ella dear, we shall see."

When Sutton had shown Lady Ella from the conservatory, the countess broke into a fit of laughter.

"Now you get the gist of that stuffy matron, Miss Hayward."

"I am sure I could not—"

"She is the same as most of my buffleheaded grandchildren. Pays more attention to propriety than having a good time in life."

"Oh, I, ah . . ."

"I know you could hear every word."

Meg had no response, so she continued to paint.

The countess rang again for Sutton. "Now, you, Miss Hayward, seem to have a happy equilibrium between your sense of fun and your penchant for duty."

"I hope I do, my lady."

"*I* hope you impart some of your ability to the earl. He is much too earnest, just as bad as his stuffy sister."

"I am afraid the earl does not hold me in high esteem. Any lessons I might offer would probably give more offense than knowledge."

"I believe his regard for you is growing higher every day, Miss Hayward. Oh, Sutton, please ask Miss Olivia to come back now."

Meg longed to ask Lady Wakefield exactly what she meant by the earl's growing regard, but she dared not. Nevertheless, the phrase echoed in her head all afternoon.

Nine

Late in the afternoon, Meg removed Nicholas's shirt, hung it on the scaffolding, and carefully climbed down. She could do no more on the sky until the paint had dried and she could see exactly how the colors blended. Not much earlier the countess had gone for her afternoon rest, and Livy had gone to their room to work on the sachet she was stitching for the countess.

Meg went to the library, chose a few volumes, and retreated to the silent morning room, where she could further improve her designs. She spread out the books of plates on the table and randomly opened one. But again she had difficulty concentrating. Her thoughts stubbornly refused to cooperate.

What was Lord Wakefield doing now? Attending to the mysterious Captain Fenton? Nor could she shield herself from refining upon Lady Ella's young acquaintance, the Lady Belinda.

Such treacherous thoughts brought her even more pain. He had to marry, of course. He was required to choose a woman to be his countess, with whom to sire sons to meet the responsibilities of his family.

Maybe she would be that duke's daughter, a lovely and accomplished young thing who could capture his fancy and change him from an austere and dignified gentleman to a cooing and pliable fellow ready to give her everything in exchange for her favors. She would dress in the height of fashion, but would she be worthy of him, as accountable for the welfare of his tenants, land, and dependents as he and his grandmama were? Would she be a conscientious chatelaine for his London house and other properties?

Meg sincerely hoped so, for it would be reprehensible if his bride was a foolish chit devoted only to society and its fripperies, a girl with an overly inflated idea of her consequence, a girl who had no notion of her place and her station, of her responsibility for caring for others.

She was horrified to feel herself wiping away a tear. Pitiful to be so nonsensical. Never mind that if her mother had only lived, she might have had a London season of her own. She might have been the incomparable that caught Lord Wakefield's eye. What-might-have-been was the gremlin of her thoughts, driving her to more and more foolhardy dreams.

Good heavens, she was in danger of dripping her tears on these lovely plates, which blurred before her eyes. She closed the volume and placed her head on her arms and gave in for only a moment to her foolish grief. Again the countess's words rang in her ears: *his regard for you . . . growing every day.* If only it were true.

"Do you not sleep well in your bed, Miss Hayward?"

So quietly did Lord Wakefield open the door that Meg jumped in surprise when he spoke. She quickly tried to hide her face.

"I fear I grew a bit drowsy," she said, fumbling for her handkerchief. She stood and walked away from the table, keeping her head turned from him as she pretended to sneeze into the cloth.

"What are you . . . oh, the Redouté roses." He re-opened the red leather cover of another book of plates. "Very fine work, do you agree?"

"Oh, very fine indeed. The detail is exquisite."

He leafed through the pages.

She took a deep breath and fought for her composure. Had he seen her work on the pilasters? Of course she wouldn't dare ask his opinion. Why would she even want to hear it? He said he cared not what she did as long as it pleased the countess.

At last she came up with a question she could ask. "Have you seen your grandmama this afternoon?"

"I just came in. I expect she is resting."

"I hope you will be considerate of her feelings, my lord. This morning she seemed most distressed about your friend."

He breathed a deep sigh and paced around the table, concern evident in his stormy visage and his agitated gestures. "I wish I knew how to handle this." He drummed his fingers on the table, then abruptly pulled out a chair and sat down.

"Perhaps you might advise me, Miss Hayward."

Meg tried to keep astonishment from her response. "Of course. I will do anything I can."

"I, ah, am sorry to bring up a topic that is beyond my right to pry, but you said your father is unwell. Or, rather, distracted mentally."

"That is no secret to anyone acquainted with our family. Ever since Mama died, he has lived more and more in his own little world, without regard for reality. 'Unsoundness of mind' is what our apothecary calls his affliction."

"I see. The term might well describe my friend's condition. How is your father treated? What medicines does he take?"

"None. My aunts brew him an herbal posset now and then, but nothing can be done to reverse the decline of his brain, or so I have learned from reading the medical journals."

"I was afraid there was no cure."

"Just the comfort and love of a family."

"In the case of my friend, his family cannot seem to help. But then, it is a different case than your father."

"Tell me more about him." Meg sat down across the table from the earl.

"We served together in the army for several years, supervising coastal fortifications in Kent and Sussex. Both of us fumed at our lack of opportunities to join the real fight. Jonathan eventually got his chance in Belgium and sadly, he lost an arm. Even worse, he is gripped by the constant need for laudanum. He says he wants only to die. If I cut off his supply, I am afraid he might try to kill himself."

Meg watched the pain in Lord Wakefield's dark eyes. He, too, suffered, seeing his friend so helpless.

"I suppose they started giving him laudanum to dull the pain. I have read it is very addictive. One lives in a sort of stupor from one dose to the next."

"I have seen much of this among wounded soldiers and even among men who have no complaint except their weakness and boredom."

She nodded. "Good food, sunshine, and activity with friends will be his best medicine. Once he is cured of his reliance on laudanum, I think he needs to be kept busy. Where has he been since his injury?"

"When they brought him back to England, his mother took him off to their estate in Kent."

"Perhaps she indulged in too much cosseting, meaning only the best, of course, but supplying him with too much of the opiate. Why did you bring him here rather than stay at his home?"

"He was a wizard at finding big, strong horses to help build the defenses. Now I want him to turn his talents to my farms. But I can hardly coax him from his bed to a couch and back. He will not eat."

"His spirits are low?"

"Very."

"Then perhaps you should enlist the countess's help. If she insists on seeing him, how can he refuse to come?"

"I fear that seeing his condition will distress her."

"More than she is already upset at the thought of being excluded from your activities just a stone's throw away? Perhaps you do not understand the depth of her love for you."

"I see your point. Thank you, Miss Hayward. It has been helpful to talk this out."

"You are most welcome, my lord."

"And, Miss Hayward, when I was in town I spoke to my man of business. I asked him to look into investing your hundred pounds if he could turn up a project he considered safe."

"You value his advice?"

"Yes, above all things. Most of my funds are invested in Wakefield, but what little I have placed in his hands has grown well."

"Thank you, Lord Wakefield."

Meg watched him walk to the morning room door, where he turned and gave her a little bow. This was the most natural and kind he had been since the incident at the lake. In fact he had treated her as a regular person, not as an impostor. He actually seemed to value her advice. Perhaps the countess was correct and his regard for her was indeed growing. The thought gave her a shiver of delight.

Meg thought the countess looked pensive at their evening meal, probably wishing her grandson were at the table. But when she stood to signal the end of the meal, she wore a broad grin.

"I want you girls to help me to my boudoir. We have some planning to do."

When they arrived, they found every piece of furniture in the room piled with a tumble of silks and satins in every imaginable shade. Sutton cleared off Lady Wakefield's favorite chair, into which he helped her. Meg gathered the fallen dresses from the floor and stacked the sofa even higher.

The countess waved a hand at the colorful array. "I had Hartley get these out from my old trunks. Some of the skirts alone will provide more than enough fabric for you gels. Now that we will soon have another gentleman with us, you need some new gowns. And I must say I am a bit tired of the two you wear almost every day."

Both Meg and Livy sputtered with opposition.

"I will abide no disagreements." The countess was not to be deterred.

Before they knew what was happening, Hartley had come in and undid their simple muslins, lifting them over their heads. Meg and Livy, both speechless for the moment, stood in their shifts, wide-eyed at the gorgeous old gowns.

"I have here the latest fashion plates," Lady Wakefield said. "The simplest of these designs will be most flattering to both of you. Your fresh young looks do not need the frills and flounces suitable for old hens like me. Try those lighter fabrics, Hartley. It is too warm for satin."

Hartley sliced the bodice and panniers off a delicious peach-colored silk and held the material up to Livy's shoulder. The hue was perfect for her.

Meg was startled out of her silence. "My lady, how can you destroy these fine gowns?"

"Hmmpf. What good do they do me inside the trunks? Hartley has already started on some new designs for me, with a proper dowager's turban and enough plumes to make everyone in the ballroom sneeze if they even approach me."

Meg could hardly summon the spirit to object again, but she must. "My lady, you are too generous, but we cannot accept these gifts. We can do with our dresses until we go home."

"Not for Nicky's ball you cannot!"

"We shall be gone days before your guests arrive. Our family is expecting us soon."

"Again I say, nonsense! You will stay for the opening of the conservatory so that you can hear everyone admire your work."

Meg's spirits took a deep plunge. The earl's birthday ball was an occasion she devoutly prayed she could avoid. She wanted to be far, far away from Wakefield.

The countess continued her insistence. "And two ball gowns are little enough reward for the pleasure of your companionship. Now, Miss Olivia, if you remove

all the trimmings from that bodice and sew them along
the hem of Hartley's new cut, I daresay it will challenge the latest modes from Paris."

Meg saw how much Livy wanted the gown, so badly
her sister could not summon the words to decline.

Meg spoke for her. "Lady Wakefield, you embarrass
us. How can we ever return your munificence?"

"You cannot, and that is a fact. So put it out of your
minds, my dears."

Meg and Livy exchanged glances.

Livy gave a little shrug. "We are entirely in your
debt."

Meg wrapped her fingers around the papery skin of
the countess's hand and squeezed gently. "We thank
you beyond what our words can express."

"Yes, my dears, I know you do. Giving you these
things and having you with me brings me more pleasure than I have had in years."

Meg knew her arguments were wasted on Lady
Wakefield, and she had to admit the gowns were
lovely. Unbidden, her hand reached toward the azure
blue of another magnificent creation. The countess
didn't miss her look, probably as avaricious as a hungry bear's, Meg thought with a pang.

"Miss Hayward, you would look quite overwhelmed
in too much of that blue. You must combine it with an
underskirt and bodice of ivory. What do you think of
that, Hartley?"

"Quite lovely, milady.

Meg stood still while Hartley took a few measurements, then held a swatch of silvery gauze under her
chin.

"Yes," the countess said decisively. "And some of
that yellow for Miss Olivia."

"Oh, no," Meg cried. "Please, not more than one dress for either of us, my lady."

The countess responded with mock harshness. "Surely you know by now, Miss Hayward, I will have my way. Your objections are of no import. You are only wasting time, and we have just a few weeks until the ball. Do you understand?"

Though Meg and Livy continued to voice objection after objection, all were waved away by the countess, who eventually sent them off to bed with her merry laughter ringing in their ears.

When she and Livy were ready for bed, Meg stared at herself in the mirror. "I find the countess the most outrageous woman in the world."

"I know. I am glad you kept objecting, Meg, because no matter how I tried, I could not tell an untruth. I want that peach silk and the yellow too. Then when she brought out the bolts of muslin, I liked them just as much. Down deep, I am a most greedy person, you know."

"I will never believe that muslin came anywhere but straight from the shops of Wallingford, despite the countess's assurance it came from the attics. As for being greedy, I cannot deny I will treasure those gowns, particularly the azure one."

"Meg, did you hear what the countess said to Hartley about the silver tissue?"

"Only that she would have her way. Did I miss something?"

"I heard her whisper to Hartley that the earl would not be able to resist you dressed in silver in the moonlight."

* * *

The next days passed quickly. Meg worked for hours on the sky before she was satisfied that the clouds were as realistic as she was capable of making them. She painted much of the background hills and trees. While they dried, she worked with her smallest brushes, carefully correcting the shading and delineating the petals on the pilaster's roses.

The earl sometimes took his morning coffee with the countess, but otherwise spent his time away from the Hall. Every day, Lady Wakefield asked him about Captain Fenton, but he cloaked his replies in carefully chosen generalities, leaving all three of the ladies disappointed.

One early afternoon after the captain had been at Wakefield for almost a week, Meg painted, Livy read, and the countess fidgeted with her stitchery, when Sutton brought a message from the earl. He sent word that the countess should expect the imminent arrival of himself accompanied by Captain Fenton.

"At last!" Satisfaction resounded in the countess's tone. "I was beginning to believe that Captain Fenton would never appear."

Scarcely a half hour later, Meg watched Lord Wakefield enter with a man leaning on his arm. In contrast with the earl's robust good health, Captain Fenton was thin to the point of being gaunt, his complexion pasty. A pinned-up sleeve indicated his right arm ended well above his elbow. His eyes stared brightly out of deep hollows, and if she had not known he had only six and twenty years, she would have guessed him to be well advanced in age.

He did his best to bow to the countess while the earl still supported him, then sank onto a chair pushed into place by a footman.

"Grandmama, I know that you remember my friend Jonathan Fenton."

The countess gave him a cheerful smile. "You are most welcome, Jonathan. I trust that you will find this sunny conservatory Nicholas has provided for me as conducive to your good health and comfort as it is to mine."

"I fear I am poor company, Lady Wakefield."

Meg did not miss the strain in the earl's face as he stepped back. He looked tense, though as handsome and well turned out as ever.

The countess waved her hand above her needlework. "Nonsense. Nicholas, make the young ladies known to Mr. Fenton, if you please."

As the earl introduced them, Meg noticed the beatific smile on Livy's face. Another needy lamb for her sister's little coterie of unfortunates on whom she could heap her compassion and gentle kindness.

Meg and Livy made their curtsies and the introductions were accomplished, bringing a little sigh of relief from the earl as he sat down beside Jonathan.

The countess was ever the gracious hostess. "The Misses Hayward have brought me a great deal of pleasure in the past few weeks, Jonathan. As Nicky no doubt told you, Miss Hayward is decorating the walls and has most recently reintroduced me to the questionable undertaking of wielding a paintbrush. Miss Olivia sometimes reads to us, wonderful novels she has discovered, and from time to time I prevail upon her to honor us with some melodies on the harpsichord. I trust you will find the young ladies an enjoyable diversion."

"I would not wish to spoil your days by my infirmities, my lady. I would not have come today if Nick had not—"

"Jon, I have known you all your life, and to infer that I ever could be displeased by your company is outside of enough. I am sorry for your wounds. To lose a limb is a great upset to the system. But you must not endanger your return to health by hiding away from those who would help you. I shall not hear of your declining to join our circle at least a few days a week. Nicholas has explained that he needs you in the stables from time to time, but that will be the only activity I will tolerate to excuse your absences from us."

Meg looked back and forth between the earl and Mr. Fenton. The earl wore the hint of a smile, and his friend must have been surprised to hear himself agreeing to come again tomorrow.

The countess was not finished. "I trust I can expect both of you gentlemen at dinner? We dine informally, Jonathan, though I promise you the Wakefield cooks are as superior as always."

The earl seemed to take in the scaffolding and the partially finished mural for the first time. "What kind of a device is that? Do you climb up there to paint, Miss Hayward?" He turned toward her as he asked, and a sudden smile of surprise lit his face. "Why, those columns are excellent. Do you see, Jon, how she has made them look round?"

Captain Fenton turned slowly and looked back and forth from one pilaster to the next. "They *are* round, Nick."

"No, they are quite flat. How have you accomplished this artifice, Miss Hayward?" He stood and came to stand beside her.

"Please do not touch yet, Lord Wakefield. Some of the paint is wet."

In spite of her best efforts to look away and appear

unmoved, she found her gaze meeting his, and she knew her cheeks pinkened swiftly. His next words brought her pulse to a pounding crescendo.

"This is fine work, very fine indeed. Do you not agree, Grandmama?"

At that moment, Meg did not care whether anyone else in the entire realm thought her painting was excellent, mediocre, or even dreadful. As the earl gazed into her eyes, only his judgment had meaning.

"Nicholas, did I not predict Miss Hayward's success?"

Instead of answering the countess, he looked back and forth from Meg to the pilasters, then uttered a muted hiss of surprise.

"Is that my shirt you are wearing?"

Meg met his glare head-on. "Yes." She wrapped her arms around herself protectively.

"I gave it to her, Nicholas. You have plenty to spare."

He continued to stare, as if cataloguing all the paint stains and smudges of chalk.

"Perhaps when I take it back, I will wear it to Carlton House and see if I can sell Prinny on a new standard of fashion."

When he at last looked away, she gripped her brush and stepped to her paints, anything to cover her quaking unease. Tentatively she took a bit of deep rose color and pretended to outline a petal. There was no denying the urgency of her need to finish soon and leave Wakefield Hall behind her.

Meg hardly stopped trembling by the time she joined Livy in their bedchamber to prepare for dinner.

"That man, that starchy prig!" Meg flopped into a slipper chair at the dressing table.

"Look," Livy said from her seat in the middle of the bed. "Look what Hartley just brought."

Meg sighed and turned, then gasped, eyeing a fluffy pile of flounces. "She has already finished one of the dresses?"

"Two of the muslins. She said the countess wishes us to wear them tonight."

"What? You mean I am supposed to prettify myself so her precious grandson can attempt to humiliate me again?"

"What do you mean, humiliate? I thought he was simply surprised to see you wearing his shirt for a smock. And his remark about new fashions was rather funny."

Meg turned away and pulled the pins from her hair. "I have a good mind to concoct the headache."

"Oh, please do not, not on Captain Fenton's first evening with us. And anyway, the earl is not a starchy prig. I think he has been all that is kind to his injured friend."

"He certainly metes out kindness in his own style."

"Meggy, how can you be so unappreciative of Lord Wakefield? He complimented your painted columns, and I noticed him watching you with a very soft-eyed look."

"What does that mean?"

"The countess and I think he is growing fond of you."

Meg dropped onto the bench. "Oh, no," she wailed. "This gets worse and worse. He is destined for a marriage of great importance. When Lady Ella was here, she told the countess of a duke's daughter whose mother practically went into a swoon when she learned an unattached young earl lived in the vicinity. When Wakefield looks at me, he sees a hired tradeswoman."

"The earl does not strike me as one who would tolerate any swooning females, no matter how high their rank."

"That is no concern of ours anyway. So you do not think I can have a tray here?"

"And affront the countess, the earl, *and* Captain Fenton? I thought you agreed to help him return to health."

"I did. But what about you, Livy? I'm surprised you are not in the stillroom, brewing up a posset for him."

"That is because I have already finished it and sent it over to Mr. Stevenson's."

"Oh."

"Now will you help me put on my new dress? I intend to look my best and try to cheer him." Livy held up a muslin gown of palest primrose yellow trimmed with a white ruffle edged with a narrow band of rosepoint lace.

Meg grinned. "You will look lovely, probably so lovely that Captain Fenton will accomplish his recovery in a single evening."

Meg could not resist holding the second dress up before her image in the cheval glass. The light shade of sea-foam green blended perfectly with her honey hair and fair skin.

When she and Livy finished assisting each other with the tapes and hooks and doing their hair with flowers Livy had picked earlier, Meg still had not figured out what her sister and the countess meant by "growing fondness."

"I think these new dresses make an amazing improvement in our looks, do you not?" Livy turned in front of the mirror and watched her reflection.

"I agree. But I do not know how we can ever repay Lady Wakefield."

"I have almost finished the sachet and I have some special bunches of lavender drying downstairs in the stillroom to put inside." Livy went to her sewing bag and lifted out a heart-shaped concoction of lace and ribbons. "I used the beads from one of the old gowns."

Meg lifted the empty sachet to the light and admired the concentric hearts Livy had embroidered in its center. "You are an excessively clever miss, sister dear."

"Why, thank you."

"And now you must explain to me exactly what you meant. A while ago you said you and the countess thought the earl was growing fond of me? Did Lady Wakefield really say that?"

"Something like it."

"Livy, do not make me yank your hair. Please tell me what she said."

"Of what possible interest could it be to you, sister dear? You just called him a starchy prig destined for an important marriage."

"Livy, you are an incorrigible tease."

"I am going down now, while my hair is connected to my head. If you still want that dinner tray, I will ask Sutton to arrange it." She flounced out the door with a quick wave.

Meg laughed as she followed her sister. "After all I have done for you!"

Ten

Nick tossed Diamond Dust's reins to Benjamin and gave the gray a pat on the neck. "The old boy was frisky as a colt this morning."

"He's got an eye for the mares, he does." Ben loosened the saddle's girth as the horse continued to prance as if yet unexercised.

"Thank you, Ben." The earl headed into the house to change out of his riding gear. On a beautiful day such as this, he wished he had some company. Jonathan had made great improvement, but he wasn't quite ready for a gallop across the fields. Miss Hayward would have loved every minute of the ride, but he had never asked her to join him before breaking her fast. Perhaps he would ask her to accompany him tomorrow.

Eason shaved him and accomplished the change of clothes with his usual efficiency.

"You are an excellent man, Eason."

"Why, my lord, how kind of you to say so."

Eason's surprise jarred Nicholas. He had to remember to thank him more often. "I may not express my thoughts often, but you know I appreciate you."

"Certainly, sir, and I thank you."

As he headed down the stairs, Nicholas thought he knew where to find Jonathan. His old friend seemed to take as much—or more—pleasure in the company of the countess and her companions as he did with Nick. For the last week, Jon willingly joined the females every morning, watching Meg paint, listening to Livy read or play the harpsichord, and talking with Lady Wakefield. His grandmama made a pet of him just as she had the Misses Hayward.

Nick tried to stay away from the conservatory. The painting project, he reminded himself, was his grandmama's responsibility. From time to time, he was rather annoyed that Miss Hayward was doing such a good job of it. Not that he wished the walls would be unpleasing . . .

Admit it, you saphead, you are envious of the way Miss Hayward and her sister have wormed their way into the affections of the countess . . . and of Jonathan.

Instead of looking for Jon in the conservatory, Nick headed for his library and slumped into a chair. From a man who had subdued his feelings for years, he was turning into a complete featherhead. His concern for Grandmama's aching joints had metamorphosed into an inexplicable attraction to a most unusual female and sleep-robbing anxiety about Jonathan's health. At least the latter problem was abating.

Jon had developed some color in his face, and he was beginning to show a bit of gumption. Yesterday he spent the afternoon looking over the seven mares and the three foals already born. His recommendation to sell one of the mares struck Nick as a sign that Jon's recovery was well under way.

Nick suddenly realized he was slouched in the chair like a miserable gangly youth. *Be honest with yourself, Wakefield. You are downright jealous of the four in the conservatory. But you have every right to be part of that group.*

He rose, straightened his waistcoat, and affected a casual saunter through the house. When he reached the door of the conservatory, Nicholas stopped and surveyed the scene.

Miss Hayward hovered over Jonathan, placing his fingers around the brush. She guided Jon's hand in a sweep over the paper. "I know it feels awkward. But soon, if you try, you will become accustomed to it and your control will improve."

Jon leaned forward but shook his head. "This feels very peculiar."

"Look at it this way." Meg held up his left arm. "This hand is free, free of all the lessons your right hand learned in school. This hand never learned the precise way to form letters or numbers. So, this hand knows no restrictions." She let go and he dipped the brush into the paint again.

Nick could hardly believe that Jon was listening to such claptrap. But there he sat, clumsily dipping his brush into the paint and swishing it across the paper. His grandmama and Livy were also engaged in spreading watery paints over their own pages.

"Good day, Grandmama, Jon, ladies." Nick came into the room and greeted Lady Wakefield with his customary kiss. "Why, you are painting, Grandmama."

"Yes, and you are standing in my light."

"Sorry." Nick moved away and turned to Miss Hayward. "You seem to have established an academy of instruction."

She handed him a sheet of paper and gestured to an empty chair and small table. "Would you care to join us, Lord Wakefield? Surely when you were a boy, your tutor must have taught you some techniques."

"I do not believe he ever, ah, my recollection does not include any painting—"

"Ha!" The countess looked up from her work. "Nicholas, I have a painting you made more than two decades ago. It is framed and hangs in my boudoir."

"The devil you say. Pardon me, Grandmama. Is that so?" Nick sat down, laid the paper on the table, and took the brush Miss Hayward handed him.

"I believe it is a portrait of your puppy."

"I had totally forgotten that."

Meg pulled over a chair and sat beside him. "Here, sir, you are holding the stem of your brush in a death grip."

Nick relaxed his hand a little, instantly eliminating the white knuckles and the feeling of strain but not even slightly ridding himself of his discomfiture. When Miss Hayward put her hand on his to guide it to the paint and paper, he felt even more ill at ease. Her flowery scent rippled around her like a halo of fragrance, making him wish he could drop the brush and concentrate on savoring her nearness, her touch. But wait, what was he thinking, almost falling under her spell again.

Innocent she might seem, to organize this little painting exercise for all of them, but she was clever. Could she have some intentions regarding Jon?

"The sky is darker overhead than at the horizon, so you want to take the blue, then make it lighter and lighter until it is very pale at the horizon."

"Yes, thank you." Nicholas was relieved when she moved over to the countess.

"You see, you are remembering." Miss Hayward leaned over the countess.

Nicholas forced his eyes away from the neckline of her gown.

"My hands won't do what I tell them," the countess complained.

"Is not the brush much easier to hold when it has the cloth wrapped around it? Making your hands obey your head is simply a matter of practice and habit."

Nick noticed how Miss Hayward fixed the brush so Grandmama could hold it more comfortably. Ingenious, he had to admit. He looked around to see everyone raptly working with their brushes.

Nick had not intended to join the group that morning, but there he sat, trying to shade a sky, and he really had no idea how he had gotten there. And he had entirely neglected his real purpose. "Grandmama, do you feel up to a visit to the fair in Wallingford tomorrow?"

"Oh, Nicky." She put down her brush. "I wish I could, but my achy joints are much too bothersome to travel that far. Why, are you going?"

"Jon and I want to look at the horses. He has some ideas about strengthening the brood mare herd, and we thought to take a look at what is being offered."

"I remember it as a festive occasion with many attractions. Perhaps the young ladies would enjoy going along."

Nicholas frowned but could hardly help responding positively without making an obvious snub. "I am sure

Miss Hayward cannot spare a day away from her painting."

The countess answered before Meg opened her mouth. "Of course she could. She and Miss Olivia should have a day to enjoy themselves."

"I cannot promise that I will have time to spare to show you around, but you are welcome to join us on our trip."

Nicholas leaned forward to dip his brush in the paint. The bottom fold of his neckcloth dangled against the wet paper and came away with a spreading blue stain.

They left early the next morning in an open barouche. The earl drove the team with Captain Fenton beside him. Livy and Meg sat facing forward and watching the backs of the men. As they passed through the village, Meg imagined tongues were wagging again, if indeed anyone was home, for when they arrived at the fair, the crowd was dense.

Crimson and blue flags waved from the top of tents. At least two dueling bands of musicians competed for attention. Dogs and children raced around the perimeter of the throng. A light breeze carried the fragrance of roasting pork and lamb. Loud voices hawked wares of all varieties, exhibitions of stupefying wonder, astonishing feats of magic, games of chance where victors would carry home a king's ransom in gold.

"We should have made some of our lemon tarts, Livy, and earned some money while we were at it." Meg stared around her, wondering where to start.

An ornate gypsy wagon carried a sign proclaiming, "Your future forecast by Madame Clairvoyant."

"I want to have my fortune read," declared Livy.

"I can do that! I predict you are about to fall in love," Meg teased. "Let's walk around first and see Madame later."

"Our first stop must be the horses," the earl said. "Do you wish to come along?"

"Yes. We always love to see the cattle."

The earl led the way through a swarm of people bearing baskets of ducklings, hens, and roosters, cages of pigeons, and bundles of farm tools. They passed an Indian rope dancer and a traveling menagerie claiming to show a two-headed calf.

When they reached the area where the horses were staked, Meg watched Captain Fenton and the earl examine a thick-necked chestnut mare heavy with foal. Her pale gold mane was neatly braided and tied with gay red ribbons.

"A fine mare." Captain Fenton began to talk with the farmer who offered her for sale.

" 'Er name's Goldie 'n she be ready to drop anytime. I cain't afford another mouth to feed, so I figger someone gets her 'n the young'un 'n breeds her right again."

Livy might have stood all day just watching Jonathan Fenton, but Meg gave her a little poke. "We can leave the earl and Captain Fenton to their business while we see what else the fair has to offer."

They agreed on a meeting time and place, and the earl gave Ben firm instructions to watch the two girls and keep them from trouble.

More likely the task would be just the opposite, Meg

thought as the young tiger looked around with wide eyes.

"Sorry you have to come with us, Ben," Meg said, "when you would rather be with the earl."

"Not so, miss. I see 'm every day. But fairs don't come my way much."

They did not progress far into the jumble of booths and stalls before they gave in to the succulent scents from the gingerbread peddler. Her fat brown men dangled from a tall stick topped by colorful rippling steamers.

"They must be delicious. She is selling them as fast as people can hand her the money."

While they waited their turn, Ben pointed at a troupe of three jugglers who grabbed the hats of passers-by to add to their whirling oranges, then tossed them back almost before the owners had missed them.

"Now, I call that skill," Ben declared.

Munching the gingerbread, the three strolled through the crowd, past a sausage stall, tables covered with large wheels of cheese, and a wrestling challenge where dozens of eager local lads lined up to scuffle with a hefty giant from the Caucasus Mountains, or so the sign said.

"Where are them mountains?" Ben asked.

"At the edge of Asia, I believe." Meg took another nibble.

"Then he's not English, is he?"

"Indeed not, unless he is really from Cornwall or Derbyshire, which I strongly suspect."

When they arrived near the gypsy wagon, Livy insisted on going in. "You must come with me, Meg, please. Otherwise I shall be too shy."

"Do you think the earl wants you t' go in there?" Ben's frown verified his disapproval.

Meg shook her head at Ben. "Oh, fiddle. The fortune-teller is probably some lass from the next village with a rag tied around her head, trying to earn a little money. You wait here, Ben. If we are not back outside in a few minutes, come call for us, please."

"I will, miss."

A swarthy man in a once white shirt appeared at the door of the wagon. "Come this way, ladies. Madame has supernatural powers that will amaze you . . . see your future for only a few pence . . ."

Meg and Livy exchanged a quick nervous glance, then followed him into the wagon. "Twenty pence." The man held out a grubby hand, Meg dropped a few coins into it, and he backed out. When a heavy black drape fell over the door, the interior dimmed. Only a candle at the elbow of a woman seated at a small table lit the space. A clear glass globe sat before her on a velvet cloth.

Meg and Livy clutched each other's hands, stepping slowly toward two chairs in front of the table. The aroma of exotic spices wafted through the air, hinting of far-off foreign climes.

"Come, sit down." The gypsy's face was shadowed by a scarf pulled forward over her forehead. The only things Meg could see clearly were the glitter of the light on her elaborate earrings and the flash of her eyes.

The gypsy leaned forward toward the girls and waved her hands over her crystal ball. "What do you want to know?"

Meg spoke when Livy merely bit at her lower lip. "How are things going at our home?"

"Mmmmm . . ." Her fingers danced in the air, sending flashes of colored light glinting onto the ball. "I see ze happy scene, ze happy child . . ."

"Child?" Livy's surprise showed in her voice.

"A young girl?"

"Two."

"Very beautiful, very bright. They are ze . . . ze sisters. . . ." The woman wiggled her fingers again. "All is well, but zey wish you home again soon."

Meg nudged Livy. *What nonsense.*

"More questions for Madame?"

"My future?" Livy whispered.

More hand movements over the globe preceded the gypsy's soft wail of delight. "I see ze man, ze strong man . . . nearby. He is dark; no, that is his friend. Your man 'as soft brown hair . . . he is searching for you, reaching out to you. Now he is waiting for ze kiss. Ah, miss, you will 'ave ze joyful marriage with this man, for he loves you forever. And ze dark man too, he learns of love but he turns away . . . he leaves your man alone to seek you . . . ah, ze image fades. . . ."

"Oh, thank you," Livy whispered. "I liked that very much."

"Send your friends to Madame."

When they came out of the wagon, Meg inhaled a deep breath of fresh air.

"What were you thinking of, going into that decrepit wagon?" The earl, clearly displeased, stood beside Ben and Captain Fenton. "Why, anything could have happened to you in there."

"I had my fortune told, and I enjoyed it very much." Livy's voice was remarkably defiant.

Meg tried to smooth over the moment. "We thank

you for your concern, Lord Wakefield, but I assure you we could have come to no harm." Meg knew her words were as nonsensical as those of the gypsy had been.

"Now, Nick," Jonathan said, "they were not in any more danger than we would have been in that tent with the two-headed calf."

Surprisingly, the earl laughed out loud. "I fell for that scam once when I was a boy. I begged to go in and after I paid my money, I could see the thing was made of painted plaster, just as my tutor warned me."

Livy tossed her head. "My fortune sounded quite reasonable to me."

"You will be shocked to hear that a romance in is her future." Meg smiled affectionately, not missing the blush that darkened Livy's cheeks and Captain Fenton's too.

"So that two-headed calf ain't real?" Benjamin asked, taking a break from chewing a mouthful of plum cake.

"No, Ben. Nor are most of the sights they want you to pay for."

"What about the sword swallower?"

"My guess is that his so-called sword is no more real than the calf."

"That's what I figgered."

By early afternoon, Meg's feet told her she needed a little rest. Livy's limp had grown more acute and Captain Fenton had lost his fresh vigor of the morning.

"How are you getting your new horses home?" Meg asked.

"Ben can lead Goldie and we'll tie the other mare to the back of the carriage. Can you take it slowly,

Ben? Or are you too full of sweetmeats to walk all the way to Wakefield?"

"I can walk, all right, but I might miss my dinner."

The earl tossed him some coins. "Get yourself a meat pie and carry it until you reach the village. Then if you are hungry, take a rest and gobble it down. But if you eat it now, I fear for your innards."

Ben dashed off in the direction of the pieman.

The earl purchased a paper cone of strawberries for them to share as they walked back to his carriage.

Meg and Livy followed a few steps behind, stopping for an instant to lick the red juice from their fingers. Two gaudily dresses females, one with a rakish tilt to her checkered hat, wiggled up to the earl and Captain Fenton. Meg and Livy slowed their steps and watched as the women sashayed around the men, bumping their hips and patting their arms.

One of the women rubbed against the earl. "Good times, laddie?"

The other tickled at Jonathan with an ostrich feather. "Methinks a good war hero needs a proper tumble, like, eh?"

Meg and Livy stared in amazement. "I have never seen such audacious carrying-on, have you?"

"Never. What do they want?"

"Money, I guess."

The men shook their heads and gestured their irritation.

"They are just like those women we saw in the streets of London," Livy declared. "Strumpets, they are called, but I am not entirely sure what they want. To rob the men, I assume, if they can get half a chance."

"All I know is that whenever I have seen such a

personage, everyone clucks at her evil ways. Yet no one ever says exactly what they do. I know only that it is very wicked."

"Perhaps we should ask the earl or Mr. Fenton."

"For a reliable answer, I suggest we put the question to the countess."

Eleven

"My lady, Livy and I have been strictly protected by our aunts from much contact with the world outside our village. Something happened today that we do not understand, and we have some questions that may be quite improper." Meg heard the little quiver in her voice.

The countess reclined on her chaise in the conservatory, having heard all about the girls' day at the fair. The early-evening sun shone through the glass walls and cast long shadows across the floor. The earl and Captain Fenton had not come back yet from the stables; the three ladies were alone.

Meg drew a deep breath and plunged onward. "Today at the fair we saw some women in gaudy clothes flirting outrageously with the men. Two of them singled out the earl and Mr. Fenton and made wicked remarks. We saw some such persons in London too, but we do not understand what they do. I know we must seem terribly ignorant."

The countess straightened up. "You poor dears. Your aunts did you no favors keeping you in the dark regarding all the terrible forms these wicked women take. You are quite right to call those women wicked. The ones you saw this afternoon are whores, women who encourage and then satisfy men's lusts. They make no pretense at being respectable. Most gentlemen find their antics quite repulsive."

"Yes, the earl and Mr. Fenton shooed them away as though they were stray hens."

The countess laced her fingers together and looked from Meg to Livy and back. "May I ask you, my dears, if you know of the love act between a husband and wife?"

Livy nodded tentatively. "You mean how a child is conceived? I know about some animals, and I know that something must occur between men and women, but I am not sure how it happens."

"Nor am I," Meg added.

The countess smiled. "That is no problem. You do not need to know the fine points until you are married. Your husbands will instruct you. But I can tell you a little about those women. Perhaps it is not my place, but young women such as yourselves need to have a bit of knowledge about these things."

"That is why we asked you. We are ignorant of so much in the world. We have heard of strumpets and mistresses, but we do not know anything about them." Meg pulled her chair closer to Lady Wakefield.

"Where to begin?" the countess mused. "Men, like the males of all species, have urges that come over them that they find hard to control. Females are rather different in that they respond rather than initiate the experience. And men can be selfish and impulsive. Since harlots give themselves to a man in exchange for money, they try to stimulate a man's baser urges. Some are streetwalkers, like the ones you saw at the fair, disgusting creatures who are sometimes diseased. Any man worth knowing will not consort with them.

"But others are more cunning in their techniques.

They find a man and worm their way into his life through flattery and shrewdness. Men are weak; they love praise and adulation, however shallow and insincere. Sometimes if such a woman becomes a man's mistress, he pays for her lodging, her clothes, even her maid. This is called giving carte blanche, for he pays all her tradesmen's bills. That makes her his property, and he can visit her whenever he wishes."

"Even if he is married?" Meg asked.

"Yes. Sad to say, many men have mistresses. And not all of them are lower class. Some ladies covet the husbands of their acquaintances. The highest *ton* is cursed with some of questionable reputation."

Livy sat, her eyes like saucers. Meg shook her head. "But if they have husbands of their own . . . ?"

"Some women look for influence over important men or like to flaunt their conquests for all to know about."

Meg looked thoughtful. "But then who is seducing whom?"

"Grandmama, what on earth is going on here?" The earl strode to the middle of the room and glared at Meg.

She wanted to shrivel up and blow away in the breeze.

"The gels were curious about the women they saw accosting you this afternoon at the fair."

"And this is a proper topic of conversation for ladies?"

"Assuredly not, my lord," Livy said quickly.

Meg's mouth was as dry as a desert. Here was Lord High-and-Haughty once more seeing her as a gawkish ninny, about as far from a proper duke's daughter as possible.

"Don't be a prude, Nicky," the countess went on. "If ladies did not discuss such things, how would they ever learn about the ways of the world? Husbands are unlikely to undertake their wives' education in the wanton ways of the wayward sisterhood, the petticoat set."

Meg spoke without thinking. "The petticoat set?"

The countess chuckled. "A wise person once told me that one could measure the importance of a subject by the number of names for it. The petticoat set is just one of hundreds of designations for the kind of women we have been discussing."

The earl looked back and forth among the three ladies. "I find the topic indecent and inappropriate."

The countess's eyes sparkled with amusement. "Why, Nicky, I was so hoping you could add to the gel's enlightenment."

"Grandmama!"

Despite her mortification, Meg clapped her hand over her mouth to keep from breaking into laughter at the earl's discomfiture.

He remained standing. "I was hoping that Jon and I could join you for dinner, but hearing your conversational choices, perhaps I am in error."

Meg looked at him straight on, hoping the tiniest glimmer in his eyes betrayed a touch of amusement. "I shall change the subject. Has Ben arrived back with Goldie? We told the countess about the fair, but we thought you might want to give the details about the horses you bought."

Lord Wakefield described the two new mares and explained how Ben needed to walk Goldie home since she was so near foaling.

When he was finished, the countess gave him an

impertinent smile. "Nicky, in what way would you say we have altered our topic of conversation this afternoon?"

After dressing hurriedly the next morning, Nicholas searched the house for Miss Hayward. The morning was fine and he wanted her to accompany him on his morning ride. Last night at dinner, her silence seemed a hushed but eloquent rebuke for his interruption of her conversation with the countess. He had never before speculated about how any young lady learned about the questionable practices of the lightskirts. Certainly it would not be the way he himself had gained his knowledge—by his experiences, both accidental and intentional.

The conservatory was empty, as was the main salon. Perhaps Grandmama was right in explaining such things to the very naive Misses Hayward.

Nicholas tried the morning room, where Miss Hayward sometimes sketched and studied books of prints. When he found the room uninhabited, he felt a sense of disappointment. But the chair was pushed back, and an open box of charcoal sat beside Miss Hayward's sketchbook on the table. Perhaps the servants had been warned not to disarrange her belongings. He stood beside the chair and smoothed his hand over the book's cover. He had no right to open it without her permission. She never offered to show these drawings to anyone, unlike the watercolor studies she painted to clarify the details of her plans.

Her work under way in the conservatory appeared to be going well. Garlands of roses decorated the pilasters that formed the load-bearing skeleton for the glass roof. One side of the wall where the glass sections were joined to the house was partially finished. He had certainly underestimated her skill.

He listened carefully for her footsteps but heard mere silence. Overcome by curiosity, he opened the book. On the first few leaves were her sketches of the lake, the bridge, and the bluebells. He turned the page and stared in astonishment. Her sketch of his face was so lifelike, he could have been glancing into a mirror. Below his face were several more sketchy versions of his entire form, one with his hand raised, as though he was leading the horses, the other staring over the lake as he stood waiting for the horses to finish drinking. He definitely underestimated her talent for portraiture.

He turned more pages. The orchids, several detailed bluebells, then a series of columns and statues, the latter probably copied from books such as she had been looking through.

The next page almost made him gasp out loud. Here was a large and intimately detailed drawing of the same Apollo sculpture that stood in his town house entrance hall. His eye was drawn immediately to the intricate and entirely accurate rendition of the male organ. He stared at it for a moment, wondering how a girl as young and apparently innocent could compose such a perfect version. But of course, he reminded himself, it was a copy, an exact duplicate of an engraving from some book. Unless she had a phenomenal memory for minutiae. He raised his eyes a little and noted the angle of the outstretched arm holding the drapery. It looked perfect. And the face . . . why, great God! The drawing's face was his!

The shock made him sit down abruptly. She had

copied the body line for line but replaced the marble features of the head with a representation of his.

He struggled to comprehend the meaning of the sketch. He did not know quite how to react, with anger or laughter, distress or indifference. Nothing struck him except the feeling of quite ridiculous absurdity. For the moment he could not tear his gaze from the page.

"Lord Wakefield!"

Miss Hayward's approach had escaped his awareness. He looked up, feeling unaccountably guilty, as if he had violated her privacy. Instead, he had discovered her complete lack of discretion.

"I do not recall giving you leave to rummage among my personal belongings." Her eyes spit fire at him.

He suspected her rage was due to the nature of the picture before him. Unless there was worse farther along. "Speaking of granting permission to assault another's belongings, I would deem one's face and limbs more personal than a sketchbook, not to mention even more private body parts."

"Those are the body parts of an ancient masterpiece, revered by centuries of admirers. Could such be called private?"

"The face is not that of the original. It looks suspiciously like someone I know."

"I was simply scribbling. It means nothing." Her face grew darker pink by the moment.

He gave her a mocking grin. "But I cannot say whether I believe the shoulders or the limbs are recognizable as mine or the Belvedere Apollo's. How would you appraise the buttocks?"

"Lord Wakefield!" Her stunned gasp revealed the

admirable accomplishment of his intention to shock her.

"How would you want me to interpret this sketch? Are you looking for a model in the flesh or are you satisfied with a marble version?"

She was not long in recovering her saucy self-possession. "Do you have a notion to strip, my lord? If so, I should have to turn over my chalks to Lawrence or Raeburn, for surely such a high and haughty personage as yourself would require a dauber of higher repute than me."

"Oh, bravo, Miss Hayward." Nicholas could no longer contain his mirth and broke into laughter.

"But for the purposes of the conservatory mural, perhaps my sketches will provide a reasonably adequate *pasticcio!*" She looked at him with a grin and an arch of an eyebrow, then whirled and marched from the room.

His laugh twisted into a strangled choke.

Meg sat on her bed and looked at the notorious page from her sketchbook. Her first reaction had been to tear out the page and rip it to shreds. But would that not give the earl too much satisfaction if he checked the book later and found it gone? On the other hand, she hated to chance the possibility that someone else might see the picture.

Her thoughts were in total turmoil. Yesterday, the earl had pointedly expressed his disapproval of that conversation she and Livy had with the countess about the strumpets and their sisterhood. How could she have been so foolish as to have asked such questions, when he might arrive at any moment?

Once the earl might have held her in high esteem—
and Livy once told her the countess said he was growing fonder of her. But that was more than a week
earlier. Now he thought the worst of her, as not only
a swindler but as an impertinent baggage who draws
a man's privates and talks about whores. The very
thought of describing herself that way made her laugh,
laughter that quickly turned to sobs.

Meg collapsed onto her pillows. For weeks now she
had refused to admit her feelings to herself. But she
could not deny them anymore. She had made the worst
possible blunder and let herself fall in love with Lord
Wakefield. How could she have done such a brainless
thing? Arrogant and overbearing, disapproving of her
every endeavor, of a status far beyond her, he was the
last man to whom she should lose her heart. Yet here
she lay, shedding an ocean of tears over the Earl of
Wakefield, over Lord High-and-Haughty himself.

From the first, she should have been on her guard.
He was too handsome, too conceited, too cold. He
seemed like the last man in the world to engage her
interest.

But his affection for his grandmama proved real.
His concern for Captain Fenton seemed heartfelt. His
interest in the welfare of his tenants and the villages
showed every day. Underneath his frosty facade he was
a warm and caring person, though he took pains to
hide that side from most people.

From what the countess had told her about the earl's
parents, Meg assumed Lord Wakefield was deeply
fearful he might become as reckless as his father, who
squandered the resources of his estate by his compul-
sive gambling. For most of his life, she guessed, he
had tried to smother his feelings, afraid they might get

out of hand. He kept his emotions under the strictest control, allowing his real feelings only the narrowest of margins. No wonder he acted so standoffish and patronizing. The man was scared witless he might let down his guard. He intended to have a reputation as perfect as the Old Earl's. If anything might threaten his character, Lord Wakefield had to squash it immediately.

She wiped her cheeks with the back of her hand and sat up again. Weeks ago he said she made him laugh. Since then she had tried to be as upright as possible, even though she had not been very successful. Since he called her a swindler, she had tried to be sincere and virtuous. Since he implied she was a hussy, she had tried to behave with perfect decorum.

In other words, she had been dishonest. She was nothing but a harum-scarum female full of contradictions. The earl was full of contradictions too, though he would never admit it.

Was love supposed to be so complicated? Here she was, mooning over the world's most impossible man. And he was afraid of love because he was afraid of himself. He would probably wed some silly chit of a duke's daughter and end up not loving her or a succession of mistresses, mistresses who took his carte blanche and put away enough money to keep themselves after he was long gone.

Twelve

Nicholas let himself into the dark conservatory. He had left the others at the card table in the salon, and he hoped they would not notice his absence. The question of the Apollo's face had pummeled him all day. But he refused to give Miss Hayward the satisfaction of seeing him inspect her murals. She would know he was checking to see if the naked Apollo wore his face. So he had to accomplish his examination in the dark.

He shielded his single candle carefully. He had to be doubly cautious, for anyone noticing a light in the conservatory at night would certainly check to see who was there. Dammit, this was his own house, his own conservatory. From the very idea to the execution, he had been in charge. Now he had to sneak around like a wretched thief, all because of Miss Meg Hayward and her fertile imagination. Devil take it, "fertile" was not the right word at all. Was every subject at this infernal place suffused with reproductive overtones?

At the dinner table he had caught himself three times staring at Miss Hayward's lovely throat, at the honey curls that brushed her bare shoulder, at the exquisite décolletage of her pale green gown. *Confound it, Wakefield, you were ogling her breasts, admit it!*

He ducked under the scaffolding and held up the candle to the wall, moving it back and forth to shed light on the charcoal sketches of ruins. Above a waterfall he found it, the Apollo Belvedere, one arm outstretched, the other placed on a broken tree trunk. He raised the candle close to the head. The face was a blank oval. Neither the original's features nor his own graced the empty space.

He quickly snuffed the candle and for a moment leaned against a supporting timber in the blackness. But he could not linger; he had been gone long enough from the salon. In his haste to leave the conservatory, he slammed his shin into another support, almost causing him to exclaim out loud. All the way up the stairs, he allowed himself to limp to ease the pain.

As he entered the salon, the card game was ending.

"Where have you been, Nicky?" the countess asked. "You missed some fine plays by Captain Fenton, though Miss Hayward and I soundly defeated Miss Olivia and Jonathan."

The earl sat gingerly on a satin chair. "Oh, I, ah, went down to look over a letter I received today. Nothing important."

"Who would like a glass of sherry? Or should I ring for more tea?"

"Sherry, by all means," Nicholas replied, gently rubbing his shin. A slight bump had already risen, and he winced when he touched it. "I will pour, Grandmama. No need to bother Sutton."

When he brought a glass to Miss Hayward, she beckoned him to lean close.

"I need a word with you, Lord Wakefield."

He nodded, served Miss Olivia and Jonathan, then came back to her.

This time she spoke in a normal tone. "I wish to

show you a picture, my lord. Can you come with me to the library?"

"Please excuse us for a moment, Grandmama."

The countess raised her eyebrows and smiled with an impish tilt to her head. "Of course."

He motioned Miss Hayward to precede him down the stairs. His mind was too occupied with wondering about the countess's strange look to prevent him from favoring his sore leg.

At the bottom of the staircase, Miss Hayward looked at him with concern. "Why are you limping, my lord."

"It is nothing. I, ah, kicked a chair by accident."

"I hope it is not serious."

"Just a nasty bump."

"I am so sorry." She led the way into the library, dimly lit by a shaded lamp. Picking up a large volume, she carried it near the light and opened it to a full-page etching of the Apollo Belvedere.

"Look, Lord Wakefield. This is the original statue in the Vatican Museum. His right arm is broken off halfway between his elbow and shoulder."

"My God! I don't think I knew that before."

"Apparently the modern copyists added the forearm, but I cannot in good conscience paint this on the conservatory walls. Even with the modern restoration, I fear it might be an insult to Captain Fenton."

Without thinking, he reached down and massaged his shin as he stared at the plate. "A good decision, Miss Hayward, if a little belated."

"Oh, no. I have not started to paint that side of the mural as yet."

"I see. Do you have an image in mind to replace it?"

"Does your grandmama have a favorite among the sculptures on the estate?"

"I do not know. But you might consider a Venus. And include your own features . . ."

She voiced a little trill of laughter. "I think I am done with putting familiar faces on statuary."

The muted light gave a glow to her complexion from her cheeks to the neckline of her gown. He forced himself to look away before he gave in to his itch to place a kiss exactly at that point.

"We had better return upstairs. I need to help the countess to her bedchamber."

She turned away to replace the volume on the shelf and walked directly up the staircase.

Nicholas and Jonathan watched the new filly gambol around her dam in the near pasture. Jed brought the news at breakfast that Goldie, the new mare, had foaled, bringing forth a prime prospect to add eventually to the brood-mare herd. Though now dark in color, she had the potential to become a golden chestnut like her mama. At the moment she was getting used to her long legs, her movements frisky, however awkward.

Jon plucked a tall stalk of grass and stuck it between his lips, where it waggled as he spoke. "She will be a beauty. Once she learns to untangle those legs."

Nicholas leaned on the fence and nodded. "Should we breed Goldie to Sultan or the big French black?"

"I hope we have four mares already in foal to the black, so I say Sultan, unless you disagree."

"Not in the least." Nicholas paused as the filly reached for her food source. The mare stretched her head around to nuzzle her daughter, who concentrated on sucking. "I'll never tire of watching that scene."

"I feel the same." Jonathan was silent for a moment, now twirling the grass in his fingers. Nick could sense his restlessness. In the past two weeks, Jon had returned almost to his old self, but yesterday and this morning he was distracted, as though something was bothering him, and he was uneasy about asking Nick for help.

At the same instant they both spoke.

"Do you have—"

"What can I—" Jon stopped with a nervous laugh.

"Go on," Nick urged.

"I have a question for you, but I do not know how to ask it. That is, I am not sure there is an answer at all."

"Yes?"

Jon drew a deep breath, then spoke so rapidly, he stuttered. "I w-want to ask Miss Olivia to be my wife. But it is p-p-probably too soon. And I have not seen my mother or sisters for a month. D-do you think she will have me?"

Nick clapped his hand around Jonathan's shoulder. *"Have* you? Why, the gel looks over the moon every time she sees you. I think she has been in love ever since you arrived at Wakefield."

"You do? With me?"

"Besides the fact you both have become captivated by romantic novels and have your brainboxes appropriately open to all sorts of dreamy notions, the situation is completely predictable. A man and a woman in constant proximity, a chaperone like the countess, who has a matchmaking gleam in her eye—what could be more natural?"

"But there is most definitely nothing to recommend me. I am hopeless. . . ."

"Nonsense. You are perfect. My admittedly limited experience with the fairer sex tells me most of them desire nothing more than an undertaking, a mission, a vocation. They want a fellow they can tend and fuss over and enchant."

"Nick! Livy would never try to cast a spell!"

Nicholas broke into laughter. "Ah, the poets say love itself is a spell you cannot resist, correct? I know you two have been supplementing those stories of knightly chivalry with sonnets about the delights of moonlight and the fragrance of roses. I would say your last few weeks have been filled with mutual enchantment."

Gradually Jonathan's smile widened and his eyes danced with excitement. "So you think she would marry me?"

"I would wager my last groat upon it."

"But my mother—"

"When Lady Fenton meets Miss Olivia, she will have no doubts about the girl's charm, suitability, and love for you. Livy's father may have attics to let. But he is still a baron, if your mother is worried about what her friends will make of it. As for Olivia, she will feel complete kinship with your mother, because they both love you."

Jon turned away, as though hiding the brightness in his eyes.

Nicholas continued. "Grandmama never wants to live in the Dower House. I'll have it done up as a residence for you and Livy. Until you fill it with a bunch of babbling brats, Olivia can come over and visit Grandmama anytime she wants."

"Brats!" Jon's voice cracked with surprise.

Nicholas could not stop laughing. "Here we are," he sputtered, "watching new life and talking about mares and stallions and breeding, and you are shocked to think you might be a father yourself someday?"

"The thought never—" Jon, too, began to chuckle. "And what about you, Lord Wakefield?"

"What about me?" Nicholas let a touch of gruffness into his tone. "I have got years ahead of me before I can start thinking about a wife."

"Why? Oh, no mind. Your life is your concern. I can only say I recommend those poems about moonlight. I appreciate your offer of the Dower House, but I first need to know if Livy will have me, such as I am."

"You are more a man than you ever were, and do not forget it. For now, go find your fair maiden and prepare for the parson's mousetrap."

Nicholas felt a great relief as he watched Jon hurry toward the house. Once he had fought off the effects of the drugs, the captain mended quickly in both mind and body. The stump of his arm had improved markedly, and his thoughts drifted in romantic clouds rather than nightmare-filled storms.

What a relief that Jon dropped his question about why Nick had not found a wife and started to fill his nursery. A similar question had been plaguing him for the past few days and weeks, surfacing in his thoughts when he least expected it. He had not planned to look for a wife until he reached the age of thirty-five. For many years he had prided himself on his ability to escape from manipulative mamas and their scheming daughters. He had not been lying when he told his grandmama he never had cared when Cynthia jilted him long ago. He had known she was calculating, cold, and selfish well before she found another victim with a plumper purse. Yet he would have married her if she had not broken off their agreement. Love had never seemed very important, nowhere near as important as family and duty and obligation.

That was the reason he felt such confusion regarding Miss Meg Hayward. It had nothing to do with that fan. She could not have been a real swindler. Her money-making attempts were really quite commendable. She was trying to help her family out of its difficulties, taking most of the burden upon herself. An admirable young lady.

Even though she had a serpent's tongue.

Meg hummed to herself as she dabbed tiny dots from her black and yellow pots of paint onto the wild-flowers at the base of the left-hand mural, the finishing details to the scene. Alone with her work, the little tune about the dell ran through her head without the words. Something about the leafy bower and the fairies, she thought. "With a hey nonny hey . . ."

The sun overhead lit the interior of the conservatory with brilliance and warmth. Meg blew a few stray strands of hair off her face as she crouched down to peer at the lowest portion of the painting.

The tiny blooms of the rock cress called for green trimmings. She arose and walked across the room for more paints just as Lord Wakefield strolled through the door.

"Good afternoon, Miss Hayward."

Meg smiled, though she wished him far away, out of her sight. For the past three days she had seen little of him and that was a blessing. Just being in the same room made her stomach topsy-turvy and her cheeks grow warm. "You will be glad to know I am almost finished."

"Please do not allow me to disturb you. Continue working if you wish."

"Thank you. If you are looking for Captain Fenton, he and my sister went out for a walk after the countess left for her afternoon rest." Meg chose a green paint pot and recrossed the conservatory to kneel at the corner of the painting.

"I am looking for you. I, ah, wonder if you can give me a progress report."

Like how soon can you be rid of us peasants, Lord High-and-Haughty, she thought. "I expect to finish the details tomorrow. Then I want all of you to examine the entire work to see if I have omitted anything."

"I see."

"For example, I think I shall paint a little grasshopper here in the teasels. And a few more butterflies."

"But that will not take you more than another day or two?"

"No more than that. Then we can be on our way home to Sussex."

"But you must stay for my birthday celebration."

"Oh, no, my lord. Livy and I have helped the countess with the lists, and we know the kind of people who are coming to your ball. And they are not for the likes of us." Particularly that Belinda person, she almost added.

"I have never heard anything so ridiculous. We will have the grand unveiling of the conservatory. You must be here. The ball is only a small part of a day filled with festivities for the whole village and all the tenants."

Meg wondered if he considered her and Livy part of the household servants, the village folk, or the gentry. "I have been away from my father and my sisters too long already. It nears midsummer and time for another cutting of the fields."

Many more days in proximity with you, she wanted to say, could break my heart. Especially while you are choosing a bride right before my eyes.

"I shall be glad to send anything you wish your family to have, whether you are worried about funds or a maidservant to lighten their load. I could even spare a man to help in your fields."

"Thank you, but there is only one, a rather small field. The man who farms the rest of the old estate property sends along some boys to cut for us. It is just that I like to be there to see they do not make the stacks too large for us to handle."

"Ah, I see."

He repeated himself, she noted, and he continued to watch her, causing her fingers to quiver and her hand to be unsteady. She tried concentrating on the tiny flowers, making each one as lifelike as possible with their subtle shadings augmented by a touch of pale green at the edges of the blossoms, a speck of brown upon the stem. But instead of her usual delicate touch, her brush seemed heavy, smearing and splattering instead of crafting realistic details.

She got to her feet and returned the paint to her table, pausing to wipe her hands on a cotton cloth. She stole a glance to see what part of the mural he was looking at, but instead, her gaze met his head-on.

Was it happiness she saw in his usually unfathomable dark eyes, or was it just the effect of the brightness? Had the strong angles and planes of his face softened, or was it a peculiarity of the light? Were his lips looking so desirable, as soft as they were the day at the lake, because the sun shone so brightly?

She felt a little light-headed, waiting for him to speak, or move, or smile, or even glower at her. But he stood in silence for a long time, until her insides shook as rapidly as the beating of a hummingbird's wings. She realized she was twisting the cloth into knots and quickly put it down, diverting her eyes from his.

At last he gave a little cough, then spoke. "I have a question to ask you, Miss Hayward. I trust it will not upset you."

Meg's mind was in a whirl, her throat suddenly dry. *Upset her? What was he saying?* She shook her head, not trusting her voice.

"You see, I look around this conservatory and I find you have done an excellent job. My grandmama is very pleased indeed. But I fear there is something missing."

"What is that, my lord?" She was sure her voice sounded like a croak of the frog she had painted on a lily pad that afternoon.

"I assume that the countess will be spending a large amount of her time here and that she will receive guests, as she has done while you were working."

"Yes?" Whatever was he leading up to?

"Up to now the furnishings have been quite temporary, carried here from other locations in the house. The effect is not particularly pleasing." He paused and looked around the room.

She did likewise and saw her table covered with a jumble of streaky paint pots and a tangle of brushes, the still-standing sections of scaffolding draped with the canvas taken up from its position on the floor. "Oh,

I assure you these messy things will be long gone before your guests arrive."

"That is not what I mean. The room calls for furniture in its own style, to complement the room, not detract from it."

Meg sank onto a chair, her knees no longer capable of holding her up. For an instant, she thought he was going to ask her to paint over the murals altogether.

"What I am trying to ask you is if you can paint on furniture?"

Meg felt her heart drop from her throat back to it customary location. She drew a deep breath. "I have painted little boxes, but never a console or a chair."

"Of course," he added hurriedly, "I will compensate you in addition to what you received for the walls."

"How much furniture are you speaking of?"

"I am not certain. Actually, the idea occurred to me only, well, recently."

Meg's heart pounded at the thought of staying another few weeks at Wakefield Hall. They could make do at home; of that she was sure. She also wanted to watch the developing connection between Livy and Jonathan, which she knew was tumbling from mutual regard into romantic love. But to be here longer, to stand by and watch the earl sort through the young ladies paraded before him? She could hardly bear the thought, much less survive the actual circumstance.

Lord Wakefield strolled over to the chaise on which his grandmama often reclined. "I suppose a table or two for tea or a lamp, somewhere to lay a book or hold a posy of flowers. Perhaps a few chairs for others to sit upon and a console near the door."

As she watched him gesturing around the room, Meg was nearly overcome with a surge of desire to be once more in his arms, to caress his cheek, to feel the touch of his lips. Just once more before she went home. Once more before she said good-bye to him forever. No matter what his high-and-haughtiness thought of her, she simply had to have a bit more time with him, enough to fill her dreams for many years to come.

She hugged his soft shirt close around her body. "If you have an old piece I could experiment on, I am willing to try my hand."

Nicholas drummed his fingers upon his desk. He found himself amazed he had come up with an idea, any idea, to keep Miss Hayward on the premises. He had stood there in the conservatory for what seemed like hours, acting like a besotted schoolboy, making her edgy and uncomfortable. Then the furniture idea simply materialized in his head like a beacon from beyond, appearing fully fleshed out—and incredibly logical. He had to congratulate himself on having more genius than he had previously supposed. Quite remarkable, if you ignored the reason he wanted Miss Meg Hayward to stay.

He pushed back in his seat and propped his feet on the edge of his desk. He had so long refused to believe in concepts like grand affection and true love, flushes of feeling that came from the heart instead of one's male equipment—or female equipment, if one was to believe the claims of a few women he had known. He had never understood why some men, as well as all females, claimed to feel more than simple regard or fondness for another person, not a parent or esteemed elder. Love, he had even claimed in several wine-soaked conversations at the club, was the invention either of lonely spinsters or mad poets looking for subject matter. One revered one's parents, respected one's elders, and would offer the protection of one's name to the female chosen to bear one's progeny. The intellect ruled over any physical or emotional involvement.

And yet he recognized some very unusual feelings these days. He had just congratulated himself on finding an excuse for keeping Meg Hayward in his house, a female he had once thought a swindler, a fraud, and a trickster. He had already succumbed to his carnal desire to kiss her, an incident he found difficult to attribute to anything consciously seductive on her part. So what were these feelings he had? Could he have been wrong all along?

When Nick was a boy, the Old Earl had often told him to admit his mistakes and defeats, acknowledge his errors, and go forward with new knowledge to do even better than before.

Would he have to eat his negative words about love? Would he have to admit to himself he was deluded?

Just yesterday Jonathan had said he never had believed it possible he could find love. But Jon had, for Miss Olivia. And she returned his feelings too.

Meg was a different story. She had been outright hostile from time to time. He liked the fact she didn't regard his every word with awe, but sometimes she was nearly antagonistic and balanced right on the edge of insult. Though how could he blame her, when he said the things he had to her.

Rude. Insulting. Yes, he had been so. Not to mention the way he had stolen a kiss and activated her indignation.

His behavior had been smug, self-important, and arrogant. In fact, if he was entirely honest with himself, he'd admit he treated her very poorly indeed in the early days. Lately they had actually had some pleasant exchanges, though he knew she thought him overly proud. But that is what he had wanted her to think.

And now? If he was developing a real tendresse for her, how did he want her to think of him?

He, Nicholas Barrington Wadsworth, tenth Earl of Wakefield, wanted Miss Margaret Hayward to adore him.

Thirteen

Meg watched Mr. Ames pick up the small table and turn it over.

"If yer gonna paint it, this finish has to come off before you start. I'll sand it down this afternoon and bring it back by three."

"And what kind of paints will I need? The same I use on the walls?"

" 'Spect so. You hafta put a base coat on it and then varnish when it's finished. Lotsa coats of varnish, I 'magine."

"Thank you so much, Mr. Ames. I could not have done any of this painting without your assistance."

"And it looks right fine, Miss Hayward."

"Thank you, Mr. Ames." Meg watched him set the table back on the tile floor, a most estimable man, dedicated to the earl and the care of his estates.

But the acquisition and preparation of furniture would take days, perhaps weeks, necessitating a longer stay at Wakefield, probably even after the birthday ball. Why had she agreed? The delay meant more days near Lord Wakefield, more torture for her poor heart, so disobedient in its insistence to be vulnerable to the earl. How could she survive without turning into a per-petual watering pot?

"Miss Hayward, I am delighted with the murals,"

the countess declared as Lord Wakefield pushed her
Bath chair into the conservatory. "I cannot imagine
anyone, even Sir Thomas, doing a better job."

Meg could not help smiling to herself. She could
certainly not envision Lawrence painting that little table!

Lord Wakefield set another pillow behind the countess's back. "My only concern is ordering the furniture
for this room. I suppose I should write to Birdsall so
he can see what is available in the London warehouses.
But, the time . . ."

"No, no, Nicky. Just go up and wander in the attics.
There are rooms full of old furniture, more than
enough for several households. You are sure to find
what you want among the castoffs of your ancestors."

"I have not been in the attics since I was a lad. May
we excuse ourselves to go up now, Grandmama?"

"Olivia is coming to read to me in a few moments.
Go ahead and see what you can find."

"Miss Hayward, Ames, can you accompany me?"

"Yes, sir."

"It will be dusty up there," the countess reminded
them.

Meg followed the earl and preceded Mr. Ames up
to the third floor. The earl carried a branch of candles
and Mr. Ames had a lantern from the kitchens.

As the light penetrated the darkness of the attic,
Meg felt like she had entered Aladdin's treasure trove,
full of trunks, old cupboards, a long-case clock, and
innumerable objects covered with white cloths. She
forced herself to resist peeking in every drawer and
under every lid.

When the earl swept the sheet off a large clump of
chairs, she coughed at the stirred-up dust. Most of the

pieces were straight-back wooden side chairs in the style of one hundred years before. But one wooden armchair appeared quite usable, perhaps even comfortable.

More furniture was pushed against the eaves, including a handsome table perfect for the spot beside the countess's chaise. Several of the consoles were potential candidates for removal to the conservatory.

The earl tested the sturdiness of the armchair and pronounced it sound. "Ames, could you gather a few men to bring these things downstairs? We need to see them in better light, but I expect some will serve our purposes nicely."

"Right away, milord." Ames immediately headed down the steps.

As the earl wandered deeper into the attic, Meg inspected a stack of old paintings leaning against a chest. The third one showed a lovely young woman with three little children gathered about her. In the faint light it was hard to make out the details of the painting, but Meg suspected it was a portrait of the earl, his mother, and his two sisters.

Perhaps, if they had hidden it away up here, she should not call his attention to it. But before she could replace it, Lord Wakefield was peering over her shoulder.

"Let me see. Why, I thought that picture had been destroyed." He took the painting and let the light fall directly on it.

Meg stood beside him. "That boy is you, Lord Wakefield. Your mama is very beautiful."

"Yes, yes, she was, though I hardly remember anything about her. This was painted only a year before she died. I was five, Ella was twelve, and Louisa nine."

He took a deep breath, as though fighting back a huge lump in his throat.

Meg waited until he was ready to begin again.

"Father took it off the wall the night she died. He said he could not bear to look at it. I thought he had torn it to shreds."

"How did she die?"

"Birthing another child, a boy who lived only a few days. Father was inconsolable. He refused to see us for many days, then he was never himself again. He turned to gambling and invested foolishly in race-horses. Everything on this estate was mortgaged to the hilt."

He stretched a hand toward the portrait to trace the outline of his mother's face in the air.

"She looks like a loving mother."

"Yes, she was. I remember so little of her really, but over the years, the stories I have heard about her seem as true as my very dim memories. I regret I did not pay more attention."

"Of course you do. But little boys do not expect to lose their mothers suddenly."

"My sisters, too, felt her loss quite deeply. Grandmama and the Old Earl always spoke of her in glowing terms, even when they were angry at my father for his wasteful habits."

Meg studied the background of the portrait. "The artist portrayed her here at Wakefield."

"She loved this house, but she died many years before my father inherited it."

"And you loved her very much."

"Yes, I did. I do. I especially remember her hugs. When she knelt down, her skirts rustled and she smelled of lilacs."

"I think we should take this picture down to your study or your bedchamber."

"It would have been there all along if I had known it still existed. Grandmama, too, thought Father destroyed it in his grief. She will be delighted." He set the portrait carefully on the chest.

Meg's heart filled to the bursting point with thoughts of Nicholas's sad loss, of the little boy he must have been. She took hold of his hand and squeezed gently. "I am so happy that you have found it."

He clasped his other hand over hers, tugged her to her feet and into his arms. "My dearest Meg," he murmured, "you are the one who found the picture. Thank you."

He stilled her response with his mouth, warm and soft on her lips, her cheek, her forehead. The scent of cedar, the flickering of the candles in the dimness, the touch of his hands, mesmerized her. She reached around his neck to pull his head to hers. As nice as his soft lips felt, she yearned to know a deeper kiss, felt an urgency toward she knew not what. But she wanted more . . . more of him.

At the sound of footsteps on the stairs they jumped apart. Meg was doubly thankful for the near darkness and the flurry of activity, for if anyone had looked closely, she was convinced her feelings would have been painted brightly on her face.

The next morning Meg found welcome refuge from the bustle throughout the house in the conservatory, alone with two prepared pieces of furniture and her paints. Every room was being turned out, polished, and organized for the coming parties. The countess and the earl had declared the conservatory off limits for the guests arriving for the birthday ball. The gardeners had even roped off part of the garden to prevent anyone peeking in from the outside.

She began by sketching a few ideas for the decoration of the little table Mr. Ames had promised to return to her by that afternoon with its base coat applied. While the earl and his grandmama were occupied with supervising the arrangements, Livy and Captain Fenton had quietly disappeared. Meg knew they had never spent any time alone, and she assumed the two were searching for a quiet retreat far from the commotion around the Hall and at the Home Farm.

Meg set aside her charcoal and began to pace the room, restlessly wondering what to make of the earl's embraces yesterday. Once they had come down from the attics, he had shown the portrait of his mother to the elated countess, then vanished from the house. Was he embarrassed by the hasty kisses he gave her? Was he staying away because he regretted his behavior? Or had the intensity of her reaction frightened him away? Why, oh, why had she pressed herself to him so boldly? Sought his lips so avidly with her own?

At last, in utter frustration, she grabbed a brush and again sought out portions of the mural that needed embellishment.

The hours dragged until just before nuncheon, Lady Wakefield came into the conservatory for the first time that day, wheeled by a handsome woman she introduced as Lady Louisa Turlow, wife of Viscount Turlow, heir to the Duke of Plobeth.

Meg rose from painting the scales on a tiny snake

almost hidden in the grass on the side of the console
and curtsied to the earl's sister.

"Miss Hayward," Lady Louisa said with a curt nod.
"Why, Grandmama, this is grand." She strode around
the room, holding a quizzing glass up to the rose-covered pilasters, as if inspecting the quality of the paint.

Meg stood quietly until Lady Louisa finished her
circuit of the room and returned to her grandmother's
side.

The countess had watched her granddaughter's
every move. "What do you think of the artist Nicholas
found me?"

"Do I want to hear that story?" Lady Louisa asked,
a touch of sarcasm in her voice.

"Perhaps not," Lady Wakefield snapped. "Miss
Hayward's talent speaks for itself."

The exchange left Meg even more in the dismals as
the two went back into the house. Just as the countess
had said, the earl's two sisters were obsessed with fas-
tidious propriety over and above manners and natural
grace such as the countess demonstrated in her every
word.

Sutton brought her a tray in the early afternoon, and
she sat alone, toying with a fillet of sole. She missed
Livy and the company of Jonathan and the countess.
Of course she could not have told them about the earl's
kisses yesterday in the attic, but their presence might
at least have taken her mind off the constant revival
of her feelings about his lips meeting hers. Amazing
how she had no control over those repetitious thoughts,
thoughts that made her cheeks warm and her stomach
flutter. After the third or fourth recurrence, she expected her face might cool when she relived his embraces. But no. If anything, her feelings grew stronger.

And no matter how many times she tried to make sense of the situation, nothing added up. In just days, the Duchess of Tetton and her daughter Belinda would arrive, and so would many more young misses, all on hand for the earl's scrutiny.

Maybe he had kissed her yesterday, but soon there would be real temptation set in his path, young ladies whose propriety matched his. Young ladies for whom a stolen kiss, if discovered, meant instant betrothal.

Obviously, that was not the way the earl viewed Miss Meg Hayward, who was merely his artist in residence, a mere minion on his estate.

But was it so simple? Yesterday she had seen a different side of the earl, a boy who had suffered the loss of his mother just as she had. He had felt real emotions when he saw the painting, however he had tried to hide them. Underneath Lord High-and-Haughty's stern exterior, he was as susceptible to his feelings as any human. And perhaps, just perhaps, could some of those feelings extend to caring for her?

She picked up her sketchpad and concentrated on her memory of the boy in the portrait. She remembered every detail, she realized as she drew, the tousled hair, the shy smile, the lovely dark eyes. She stared at the face for a long time, then flipped the page and drew the same portrait all over again. She needed one more short viewing of the painting for a few quick amendments to her work and she would have two versions, one for Lady Wakefield and one for herself to keep forever.

"Actually, Miss Hayward found the painting in the attic," Nicholas told Louisa.

She wiped a tear from her eye. "I am so happy to see it again after all these years. We were so happy, were we not?"

"Yes, we were." He fought back an urge to join in his sister's tears. "Grandmama is delighted and wants to hang it in the dining room."

Lady Ella joined her siblings. "I want to send it out to be copied. I want to have an exact replica for myself, and I am sure you do too, Louisa."

The earl backed away from discussing the choice of artist's studio for the assignment. He hoped the meeting he had called here would not take long, for he wished to have a few moments alone with Miss Hayward. All day, a constant stream of tasks had kept him away from the conservatory and drove his frustration almost to the breaking point. It was so unlike him to be annoyed by his responsibilities, almost as unusual as his spontaneous embrace of Miss Hayward in the attic. He ran his fingers through his hair, spoiling the arrangement Eason had carefully created. Why did so many of his cherished values lately seem irrelevant and totally outdated?

Miss Hayward came into the room arm in arm with her sister, giving his heart a jolt. He went to them, leading them to a sofa near Lady Wakefield. His action and the warmth of her welcome ought to give Louisa and Ella a better idea of the regard which they should have for the Misses Hayward. But he had time for only a warm smile for Meg once the girls were settled.

When Mr. Stevenson, Sutton, the housekeeper, the cook, and the estate supervisors came into the drawing room, Nick addressed them all.

"Lady Wakefield and I want you to know how much we appreciate the efforts you are making to prepare for the festivities. The next four days will be busy for all of us, but the ultimate goal is for every person, whether a guest here at the Hall or at the celebration outside, to have an experience worth remembering."

He enumerated the various events leading up to his birthday and finished by presenting the final schedule. "Lady Wakefield's guests will dine at the Hall on Wednesday night. On Thursday, Lady Wakefield will receive her guests in the conservatory for an hour before some of the young ladies entertain at a brief musicale before dinner. Meanwhile we will open the conservatory to everyone, all our tenants, the estate workers, and village residents."

His words brought smiles and nods of satisfaction. He stole a glance at Miss Hayward, who wore a broad smile.

"Lady Wakefield, the vicar and I will then join in a feast for everyone on the south lawn to be followed by a dance. The musicians are coming from Wallingford for the occasion."

Once more he heard a chorus of admiration. "And once the banquet is under way, the vicar will come back with us to the Hall to bless the dinner here, with a ball to follow. If everyone is prepared in advance, we will not need any of the servants here. We will serve ourselves and let everyone go to the party."

His final words brought a hearty round of approval.

Nicholas found himself held up by a flurry of questions and missed Meg's departure. Instead of going after her, he had to go outside to show Mr. Ames just where his workers should construct the musician's stage.

By the time he returned to the Hall, he found Miss

Hayward had retired for the night. His proposal would have to wait.

For the next two days Meg enlisted the help of Livy and Jonathan to complete the furniture for the conservatory. Jon declared himself proud of his ability to fashion a tree and adorn it with green leaves, and all with his left hand. She did not dare to tell him so, but Meg was certain that soon he would be able to control his left hand well enough to practice writing. Livy, clad in one of Jon's shirts as her smock, painted dainty flowers on graceful stems and arching branches of delicate apple blossoms on Jonathan's trees.

Lady Fenton's arrival on the morning before the festivities took all three of them by surprise.

Sutton had barely announced her name, when a woman in a lavender pelisse ran toward Jonathan, calling his name. When she saw him on the floor, his shirttails in disarray and his face streaked with brown paint, she shrieked in bewilderment. "My darling boy, what are you doing?"

"Mother. We expected you later in the afternoon."

Explanations were lost in her tears as she hugged her beloved son looking the picture of good health, if untidy in the extreme.

Livy, whose intention of appearing all that was proper as she had been elucidated to Meg in excruciating detail, stood gaping at Jonathan and his mother with a painful pucker to her lips. Meg put her arm around her sister's shoulder. "Give her a chance to recover and everything will be fine."

Livy only sighed.

At last Jonathan extracted himself from Lady Fenton's grasp. "May I make known to you Miss Hayward and Miss Olivia Hayward. Miss Olivia is the one who took down my letters to you."

Lady Fenton hugged Livy, then Meg, spilling her tears on both of them, until they led her to an unpainted chair, where she could recover her sensibilities.

"Jonathan, you are so much better than I ever could have imagined. The earl must have wondrous hygienic waters here at Wakefield or a miracle-working physician on hand."

Sutton reappeared to escort Lady Fenton and Jonathan to the countess, and as suddenly as the whirlwind had blown up, it was over. Livy and Meg were alone together.

Meg gave Livy another squeeze. "Off to change, sister dear. The next time Lady Fenton sees you at nuncheon, you will look your very best. I will be along in a moment to help with your hair."

Meg declined to change her own clothes and interrupt her final day of painting any longer than it took to do Livy's hair. She returned to the conservatory to put finishing touches on the last of the furniture.

In midafternoon Livy came to report three carriages full of guests had arrived. One held Lady Dornyngton and her three daughters, all seemingly among the eligibles brought to exhibit before the earl. According to Lady Wakefield, there were at least seven young ladies, some with great beauty, some with great dowries, some with great bloodlines, but few with great wit.

"After she met them, the countess told me she was disappointed." Livy mimicked the countess's voice and manner. "In my day, young ladies were expected to have a bit of conversation, not just lisp and giggle, as those chits did."

Meg's hands were clenched into white-knuckled fists. The only time she had seen the earl that day was from a distance, and her expectations of their talk had crumbled into dust.

She was not surprised to find herself seated far down the table from the countess and the earl at dinner. Upstairs, she and Livy had preened before their mirror, congratulating themselves on their fashionable appearances. But among this company, their new gowns were most notable for their simplicity.

Lady Fenton told all who would listen of her son's remarkable recovery. Jonathan, however, had eyes only for Livy.

As soon as she could get away from the ladies after dinner, Meg tiptoed to the conservatory and let herself in. Darkness had not fully descended, and she could easily see the details of the murals, the pilasters, and the grouping of furniture. That afternoon, men brought a wagonload of plants from the orangery and placed them around the walls, completing the effect the earl had originally planned for his grandmama.

Well, almost, she thought. Lord Wakefield never planned to have the walls painted with murals. She admitted to herself they turned out much better than she once anticipated. The sense of perspective worked well, from the distant trees moving forward to the lake, the bridge with the figures resembling the Old Earl and his countess early in their marriage as painted by Gainsborough, and forward to the base of the painting, where things were close enough to touch in life size.

Here was where she had done the orchids, some insects, especially butterflies, and a nest of baby hares.

When she heard the door open, she assumed Livy had come to take her back to the drawing room. But when she turned, her companion was Lord Wakefield.

"I suspected you would be here," he said, walking toward her with a smile, his voice light and his manner genial.

She simply had to get away from him soon, or she would be forever lost to unanswered love. He was so very handsome, so very tempting.

"Are you happy with your painting, Meg?"

His use of her given name made her wary. The last time he had done so was in the attic, and look where that had led. She could not afford another wrench to her heart. She stepped away from him and toward the mural.

"I see several places I wish I could redo. There, under the beech tree, for instance—"

"Why? I say it looks perfect, and the countess is ecstatic. She can hardly wait to bring in all her guests tomorrow for the grand introduction. And she has not seen the greenery and flowers in place."

"I can only hope no one else notices the mural's shortcomings."

He moved to stand beside her. "What shortcomings?" He held up a hand and spoke quickly. "Do not give me a list of things you wish to alter. You have often accused me of being puffed up in my own self-importance, so I will fulfill your description by declaring the mural without peer in the realm. It is perfect if I declare it so. Now, do you see how useful a sense of self-importance can be?"

His voice was tinged with suppressed laughter, and

she stole a glance at his face. In the darkening half-light, their eyes met with an intensity that belied his lighthearted words.

"I hope your guests will find it pleasing."

"As long as Grandmama is happy, I care not what others might think, though I predict the shared verdict will be on the level of a masterpiece."

"Oh, Lord Wakefield . . ." Her heart skipped a beat as he moved close to her and took her hand.

"I have a confession, Meg. In my heart I never considered you a swindler. It was my embarrassment at buying the fake fan that caused me to be so offensive to you. I regret . . ."

At the very moment she told herself to run for her life, Meg felt drawn by an irresistible force. She leaned toward him and met his lips with hers.

Entirely enfolded in his arms, her hands found his shoulders, gradually creeping around his neck. The kiss deepened and she spread her fingers into his hair, hearing his moan and feeling his arms tighten. Their bodies pressed together so closely, she could feel the fob at his waist pressing into her. The kiss went on and on, touching and probing. Meg could not have forced herself to pull away for any reason on earth. This felt so very right, so very perfect. Every muscle, every nerve within her, sang in harmony.

When at last he drew his mouth away from hers, he whispered to her, little words of desire and longing. "My darling . . . my sweet . . . my cherished one."

Meg was speechless with wonder. The stolen kisses she had almost come to expect from the earl, but such endearments? Impossible! He was the man who did not believe in sentiment, in emotion, in love. He was the man who declared that affection should be reserved for the family, passion for those baser moments, adoration for misled poets and lady novelists; devotion he reserved for God.

"My dearest Meg," he said, raising his head from nuzzling at her neck. "I cannot let you go."

She shook her head, but he tightened his grip on her again and rained kisses on her forehead, holding her still. "You must stay and be mine, here with your sister and Jon, with Grandmama and everyone at Wakefield. I will care for your family and they shall want for nothing. Say you will stay, my darling."

She could not believe her ears, trust her jumbled thoughts. Nor could she deny the melting sensation filling her body, making her hold on to him as tightly as she could.

For a long time their lips were engaged and she could not speak, nor did she want to. Then tears came, unwelcome, spilling down her cheeks and wetting his lips.

"I am sorry," she whispered. "I am so silly—"

"It is I who should be sorry. You are exhausted; you have worked too hard. I asked too much of you."

"No, it is not that at all."

"I will see you upstairs so you can rest. We can talk more tomorrow."

He took her arm and started to lead her from the conservatory. "You have not answered me, my dear. Will you stay at Wakefield? Please?"

She could answer only with a sob, though her heart was calling out so many questions. How long? Forever? But her voice refused to cooperate.

At the staircase, before she could say a word, he took her in his arms again and kissed her breathless.

Every drop of blood in her body seemed effervescent, as full of sparkly bubbles as the finest champagne.

"Do you love me, Meg?" he murmured against her cheek. "Say you do."

"I am overwhelmed. I cannot think anything at all right now. My head is a muddle."

"Nicholas!" a voice called from the drawing room.

"Damnation," the earl muttered.

"I shall talk to you tomorrow," she whispered.

"Sleep well, my sweet Meg."

He held on to her hands and kissed her fingertips as she turned and headed up the stairs, her eyes brimming again with tears.

In the quiet of her bedchamber, she flung herself across the silken counterpane, her face pressed into the pillow. The strain of the past week was almost beyond endurance, and she wanted to do nothing but to sink into the soft mattress. But her mind would not allow it. Filled with swirling thoughts and whirling images, her thoughts careened from here to there and back again at dizzying speed.

Lord Wakefield—Nicholas—wanted her to stay at Wakefield. He needed her, he said. He asked her if she loved him.

But did he love her? Had he said the words or were his kisses evidence enough? He would care for her family, but what did that make her?

He had not mentioned the word marriage. Or wife. Abruptly she rolled over and sat up, clasping her knees to her chest.

He could not have meant he expected her to be his mistress. Certainly not. Such a thing was unthinkable.

She tried in vain to recall every word he uttered. Had he said he loved her? Not that she could remember. She was sure he had not mentioned marriage or betrothal. And somewhere under the sprawling roofs of this great mansion lay a half-dozen young women who wished to receive his proposal. Not one of them or their mothers or their brothers would believe the earl would take to wife the penniless daughter of an addlepated and reclusive old baron who hadn't been to court for at least a dozen years.

There was no doubt about it. The earl, damn him, had offered her a carte blanche! His lordship had presented her with the opportunity to become his paid mistress. Meanwhile, he could have a wife and family at home.

But did Nicholas, with his seeming change of heart and mind about love, intend to acquire both a mistress and a wife at the same time? She had a very hard time imagining that a man who embraced her so fervently tonight would betroth himself to another tomorrow.

Without resolving the quandary, she fell into an exhausted but restless sleep.

Fourteen

Nicholas found the activities of his birthday almost intolerable. He attended to myriad duties, responded to countless obtuse questions, greeted dozens of guests, some of whom claimed to remember him since the cradle. An endless line of young ladies curtsied to him, each more deeply than the last, until he almost wanted to grab Lady Belinda Tetton before she slapped her forehead on the floor and fell into a swoon.

At nuncheon, the dining room was jammed full of females of all ages lying in wait, competing to dominate his time at the table with empty compliments, silly remarks, foolish guessing games, and apocryphal stories of their ancient forebears. He had never eaten so rapidly in his life.

By midafternoon he realized he had not seen Meg all day. And now, as he stood in his dressing room and gave a final tuck to the ends of his precisely tied neckcloth, he looked forward to having her positive answer to his proposal. He wondered if he should ask his grandmama to announce his forthcoming marriage just before the midnight supper.

He stood for a moment while Eason brushed his coat. The announcement of Jonathan and Livy's betrothal was the one bright moment in his day. Lady Fenton never appeared so relieved and carefree. Her congratulations made him chuckle inside, because in many ways he himself had changed almost as much as had Jonathan. The more he thought about it, the more he liked the idea of marrying very soon; in fact, the sooner, the better.

He ran his hand over his smooth-shaven jaw. He had always felt the pull of duty, even when he was a youth. All because his father lost interest in the estate after his mother's death, turning to gambling, horses, and wasting his blunt on a series of greedy mistresses.

The Old Earl had been terribly disappointed in his only son, saying Richard suffered from the faults of men given to an overabundance of unbridled emotions, who let their lusts take over their heads. Years later, when the Old Earl passed on, it was his father's recklessness that nearly depleted Wakefield's resources.

Nick had always avoided the trap of emotionalism, yet now it seemed natural and inevitable that he would become a believer in love. What it took was the right female. He supposed he ought to thank his lucky stars Meg was not a grasping, chattering cabbagehead like some of his guests. He liked her streak of independence. She did not peep from behind a fan or flutter her lashes as if she had a cinder in her eye. Or lispingly offer to fetch him another treat from the side table when he had just seated himself with a full plate and had several servants tending to his every wish.

At the ball he might not have much time to spend with her, but he wanted to be in her thoughts every moment. Perhaps he could take her the repaired fan, but he would rather save that for later. *Ah, the perfect solution!* His mother's earrings. Since childhood, he had kept them tucked away, and as soon as he could remember their exact location, he would take them to Meg.

* * *

Meg could find nothing that needed her attention. The conservatory was finished and closed up until later. She had made a little cardboard frame for her sketch of Lord Wakefield's face as it appeared in the portrait.

The countess and her grandson were receiving their titled guests and Livy was inseparable from Captain Fenton and his mama. The last thing she needed was to go downstairs and find herself swept into some group walk or game with those brainless twits or their mothers. In her bedchamber, she had read twenty pages of the novel on her bedside table but did not remember a word.

Sighing, she picked up her bonnet and tiptoed to the back stairs and out through the busy kitchen wing, well populated with visiting servants. As she skirted the grounds of the Home Farm, she could see five men building a platform for the village dance that night. Near the river, she heard laughter ahead, and cut away into the woods that flanked the lake.

Near a huge beech tree she sat and leaned back against the smooth trunk, wondering for the thousandth time that day what the earl meant last night when he asked her to stay with him, to stay at Wakefield Hall. Would he have gotten around to mentioning marriage if she had not started to weep like a ninny? Her ridiculous reaction to his questions might well have made him reconsider. What did he need with a rag-mannered peagoose like her? Did he simply want a permanent companion for Lady Wakefield? These were the questions that haunted her dreams and ruined her sleep last night and filled her thoughts all day.

One thought remained constant, however. She would rather give him up and regret it all her life than see him every day if he took another to be his wife. She might spend the rest of her life wishing for what might have been, but she could never survive the pain of seeing him as the husband of another.

She had no more tears. No more emotions to inflame. No more pretense to probe. She felt numb and empty, stripped of all defenses. Alone, tired, and helpless . . . lulled into a restive doze by the dappled sunlight and gentle buzz of insects.

When she awoke, Meg had to hurry back to the house in order to be on time for the opening of the conservatory. She had barely enough time to change. Whenever would she and Nicholas—or had she better refer to him as Lord Wakefield in view of her questionable status in his future—find time for their little talk? Until she knew what he intended, how could she answer his question?

The house was silent yet seemed filled with a great sense of anticipation, as though suddenly all doors would burst open and the hallways spill out dozens of people all trying to outdo one another in beauty, charm, wit, and fun.

Nevertheless, she asked herself as she ran up the stairs what would she answer Lord Wakefield if he proposed marriage? If he proposed she stay here and become his mistress, tucked away from a wife and his presumed heir? Somehow, despite her complete inexperience, she thought she knew exactly how such a relationship would be: she would stay on the outskirts of his life, watching his lady wife and his children from a distance. No matter how much he declared he loved her best, that would be a life of grief and sorrow, not a life of comfort and ease. A life of loneliness, yearning for her own child, her own station in life.

Back in her room, she was alone again. Livy was nowhere to be seen, though some evidence of her recent occupation could be seen from the pile of stockings on the chair to the glove box tipped on its side on the dressing table.

Meg swept the stockings onto the floor and plopped herself down. Better she never see the earl again than to see him achieve fatherhood with another woman. She glanced at the bed, tempted to crawl in and let the party go on without her. A small velvet box, like nothing she or Livy owned, lay in the center of the counterpane.

A note accompanied it: *To dearest Meg, Please wear these tonight. N.*

Inside were diamond earrings, sparkling brilliantly even in the diffused light of the bedchamber. He brought them for her to wear. Did this not mean he loved her?

Yet she remembered how the countess said gentlemen bought their mistresses—the ones they gave carte blanche—many pieces of jewelry to keep them happy.

At the scratching on the door she grabbed the box and the note and stuffed them under the pillows. "Come."

"Miss Hayward!" Hartley's voice was disapproving. "Here you are, unprepared for the presentation, not even dressed, when milady is ready for you downstairs. Here, let me help you out of those things."

Meg gulped back her urge to rebel and stay right where she was. With Hartley's capable help, she was soon changed, clad in her new gown and slippers, her hair caught up high with matching lace and ribbons.

Hartley made her turn in a circle before the mirror. "Look, miss, did y'ever think you'd look so handsome?"

"No, indeed, I did not. You must be the finest seamstress in all of England."

Hartley surprisingly broke into a big grin and her cheeks flushed pink. "Thank you, miss."

"But do you not think I ought to tuck a bit of silk into this neckline?"

"Wait till y'see the tiny tops on some gels. Seems like young ladies are purty eager to show their charms these days."

"Not I! I feel rather bare. But you hurry off now and get ready for the party yourself. Thank you again. I will go down in just a minute."

"The countess will be waiting." Hartley's voice carried a warning tone as she left the room.

Meg grabbed the earring box from under the pillow, opened it, and carried it to a shaft of sunlight. The two stones flashed fire-sparks of crimson and azure, gold and turquoise, as she wiggled the box in the sunlight. What did this gift mean? If only something would clarify the earl's intentions . . .

A man like him, a peer of the realm, would never choose a country nobody like her for a countess. The very thought was ridiculous. Not that she could not be a credible countess. She would model herself after Lady Wakefield, with concern for her family and her tenants foremost in her mind, not the fripperies of the social scene. Why, yes, Meg thought, she could be a very fine countess indeed.

But Lord Wakefield would never think so. Never in their many conversations, never before or after their several embraces had he apologized for calling her a swindler. Perhaps he still thought she had tried to trick him. That was the very first question she would ask when they had their promised talk.

Meg dropped the box and the note into the reticule Hartley had made of scraps left over from the bodice of her dress. And thinking of that bodice, she gave it a tug upward and hoped it would stay where it belonged.

Nicholas excused himself as he made his way through the clutch of people gathered in the saloon in front of the shuttered conservatory doors. The Countess of Wakefield planned her ceremony for maximum dramatic effect.

As he joined his grandmama, Nick felt his heart jump and his breath shorten at the sight of Meg standing next to the countess. She looked transformed, like a fairy princess. Her new gown seemed made of silver shimmering in the late-afternoon sunlight. She looked so delicious, he was tempted to sweep her into his arms. But why was she not wearing his earrings? His initial elation darkened with alarm.

The countess placed her hand on his arm. "Are we ready?"

"Indeed." He had eyes only for Meg, and they exchanged a fleeting glance before her eyes darted away and fixed firmly on a distant target.

"My friends," Lady Wakefield said. "I am proud to show off today the latest in conservatory designs which my grandson had built for me. Though this is his birthday, he has given me this wonderful gift. And he even brought me the wonderful artist, Miss Margaret Hayward, to decorate the walls and furniture. I myself have not been inside for over a week, and Nicky hints that I will find some surprises. Please, let us go in."

Sutton swung open the doors and Nick half carried his grandmama inside, followed by Meg and a gaggle of guests, all exclaiming at once. As he watched the wonder in Lady Wakefield's eyes, Nick knew he had never done anything that gave him more satisfaction than to see this project to completion.

The countess looked about the room, from the completed murals on either side of the door, to the handsome containers of lemon and orange trees, to the jardinières filled with tropical blooms, to the fancifully painted chairs, tables, and the console.

"Nicholas, it is wonderful. I have no words superlative enough to tell you how much I love it!" Lady Wakefield reached up, kissed him, and hugged him close.

"Grandmama, I loved every minute of watching it take shape."

Nicholas and Sutton helped the countess to her chaise, and she was quickly surrounded by guests full of questions.

Meg was the center of a group, all seemingly talking at once. He watched her for a few moments, almost uncomfortable seeing her in the unfamiliar garb of a sumptuous ball gown instead of the muslin topped by his old shirt for a smock. How strange, he thought, that he preferred her in her working clothes. Even though the new dress's neckline was modest by the standards of many a lady's décolletage, and he certainly enjoyed the view of her bosom's gentle swell, he had grown to appreciate her everyday looks. Her hair and gown were quite lovely, yet dressed in such finery, she hardly seemed like his Meg anymore.

Abruptly he realized several people were speaking to him, and he had no idea what they were talking about. He smiled and excused himself, but he could not escape a clinging mama and several young belles, his way to Meg now blocked. He would have to wait to speak with her until these guests departed for the musicale.

But when that time came, the local villagers and tenants were already waiting to enter the conservatory to greet the countess and see her new indoor garden house. At least, Nick thought, in this crowd he would not have to dodge the silly widgeons who wanted to trap him. When he got a rare glimpse of Meg, she seemed engaged by her conversations with the village women and children. Mr. Ames sang the praises of Miss Hayward and she exaggerated his role in the preparation of the walls and furniture.

Long before everyone had their fill of the conservatory, it was time for the earl and his grandmama to join the vicar in opening the grand feast on the lawn. Nick managed to speak to Meg for only a moment.

"Your murals have earned praise from everyone, even the blacksmith."

"People have been very kind."

"I hope you will reserve a dance for me later."

She shook her head, as if refusing. "You will be surrounded with your guests."

"But you promised we could talk this evening." He feared she might have forgotten. "Did you find my earrings? You are not wearing them."

"I cannot accept your gift. At least not until you answer a question."

"Anything you ask—but that will have to be later, I am afraid. I must go now."

"I know."

"I will meet you in the garden near the seahorse fountain at an hour before midnight."

She nodded, unsmiling.

As he moved among his tenants, talking to their families and admiring the new babies from the village, half of Nick's mind occupied itself with trying to figure out what she wanted to ask. He considered it ominous that she would not accept the earrings. He only wanted her to look her best, and he knew she had no jewelry of her own. What would keep her from accepting them?

At last he and the countess returned to the Hall for their dinner party and the ball.

"We have set ourselves a sprightly pace today, Grandmama," Nick said.

"Reminds me of the old days. Festivities like this happened every season. I can sleep when I am in my grave."

"Not that you will have any choice then."

She laughed, for he knew exactly the kind of remark she liked, the kind the Old Earl would have uttered.

He only caught glimpses of Meg in the next two hours. She was usually the center of conversational groups and she spoke animatedly, now dispensing smiles in all directions. Indeed, his might be the only proposal to which she did not respond tonight. He chuckled to himself at the thought but felt no real mirth.

Unfortunately his pause to study Meg and her fellow conversationalists caused him to be cornered by Mrs. Symonds and her dreary daughter, Miss Elise. He could not escape a dance with her, one of the least attractive of the young ladies in attendance. As they took the floor, he forced a look of good humor to his face.

For a man who long prided himself on his devotion to duty, no matter at what cost to his patience, this day was becoming a purgatory he feared he might never leave. For most of the last four hours he had been in the same room with Meg, but she might as well have been at the Land's End tip of Cornwall while he was in the Shetland Islands for all the time they had spent together.

Meanwhile, Meg had long ago wearied of questions about her paintings and the conservatory. She had no idea what to say when she was asked about future commissions. She clung to the hope, so very foolish, she feared, that the earl's words yesterday might have been a marriage proposal, not a proposition to establish her as his fancy piece.

She watched him lead out several young misses, including some of remarkable unattractiveness or with perversely overdone ensembles—or both. Those ingenues were probably the ones with ample dowries, the kind who would eventually drive any husband to the arms of a mistress, no matter how immoral it was.

Why, Meg, she scolded herself, what a dreadful turn your thoughts have taken!

The brightest spot in the evening was Livy's radiant happiness, and her good terms with Lady Fenton. Actually, Meg did not wish to be selfish, but she would miss their chats. Meg chided herself a little. Was she the tiniest bit envious? Perhaps. Anyone could see Livy and Jonathan had openly avowed their love and joyously faced the future.

Meg, on the other hand, felt all at sea. She could hardly declare her feelings until the earl made known his intentions. Why was it so complicated? Because she had firmly disliked Lord Wakefield from the start, had baited him, had teased him, had called him pompous and haughty? All that time she had been anything but immune to him. Even when he called her a swindler and a fraud.

She had allowed him to kiss her more than once, and she had kissed him back in a way she was certain an innocent young woman would not. She had stared at the private parts of that naked Apollo, even sketched it with Lord Wakefield's face. How could she imagine that he thought her anything but a jade, a woman of loose habits and questionable standards. Once he had talked of tossing her, and Meg knew his inference was something quite wicked.

She painted a smile on her face and tried to look responsive when people spoke to her, but her mind was far, far away. How could she measure up to his standards? He was born to the role, and though she had been born to it also, circumstances had turned her life in other directions. Toward gathering eggs, planting turnips, and painting fans to help her family. He would not, could not, make her his countess.

She tried to observe the ladies carefully. She ought to write down some of their capers, for she was sure tomorrow she would never believe some of the affectations she saw. After all, she had to instruct her sisters, Bea and Dorie, and she knew they had never seen anyone acting quite like this. These young ladies cooed to each other as if addressing a newborn kitten. They giggled as if being tickled by an ocean of ostrich plumes.

As she watched the dancers, she decided to set aside some of the money the earl paid her for painting the furniture to hire a dancing master for her sisters. Some of the steps looked rather complicated, and although she and her sisters knew a few country dances, it was clear the girls would have to be better prepared to shine in company like this, not to mention to keep from tripping over their partners' feet.

Time after time, she consulted the clock in the green drawing room. At last, her heart hit new heights of hammering as she noted she should leave for her rendezvous with the earl at the seahorse fountain.

Nicholas excused himself from Sir Busby Duckworth and slipped out a side door of the ballroom. Without checking his timepiece he was certain the hour of eleven approached. He had maneuvered himself to be near the door when the time arrived for his meeting with Meg. He patted his tailcoat pocket to be sure the package was safe.

Avoiding the regular paths, he cut across the grass, fearing he might again meet up with guests and be detained by more congratulations. He stayed in the shadow of a high yew hedge since the moon was full, the evening warm, and many strollers enjoyed the garden.

The day had passed with aching slowness, yet he felt unprepared. He wondered again what questions she had and how his answers might affect her acceptance of the earrings, of his proposal.

It was unlike him to feel his nerves so acutely. He prided himself on his courage and resolve, but that was before he had been overtaken by these strange feelings he could call only his emotions, the side of himself he had long buried. Now he was lost, had no anchor. All was new and different and trying. He had spoken in the House of Lords, but the thought of speaking to one young lady to ask for her hand stifled his thought process and dried out his tongue. The feeling was unfamiliar, his reactions strange, the whole experience unlike anything he had ever experienced.

Meg sat on the edge of the fountain, staring downward and dabbling her hand in the water. He drew a sharp breath at the sight and felt his pulse race. In the moonlight, she looked ethereal, like a figment of his imagination, all silvery and fairylike.

When she looked up and saw him, her smile had a tentative cast that made Nick even more apprehensive. What he wanted to do was run to her, gather her in his arms, and kiss her senseless. But he kept himself under what little control he had left.

"I thought I should never make my escape," he said.

She stood and faced him. "You are the center of the day's festivities, my lord. No one could imagine you wanted to leave."

"But I did. All day I have wanted nothing more than to be with you, alone for even a few minutes, yet we hardly had a chance even to set a meeting place."

"True."

"I promised to answer your questions about the earrings."

"Why did you give them to me?"

The very simplicity of her question stunned him. "I thought they would make you even more beautiful and I wanted to make you happy." She was silent and he stumbled on, hardly knowing what direction to take. "You have sometimes spoken of having few luxuries in your life, and it is my pleasure to provide you with some. I hope that in a few months, you will have more jewels and gowns than you can imagine."

He stepped toward her and reached for her hand, but she turned away to look again into the water. The water splashed gently and the light danced on the rippling surface of the pool. This was the kind of scene lovers were supposed to find inspirational, evocative of love. But he, Nicholas Wadsworth, was inarticulate. The words he ought to be saying just did not come.

At last she spoke, still staring at the water. "I cannot accept your gift. I have my family to care for."

Here was a subject he thoroughly understood. "I understand your obligations, and I honor them. Your concerns speak well of you, Meg."

"Then you understand why I must return home."

"No, I fear I do not. I will care for all your family. If you worry about your father, you may bring him here to live at Wakefield. Or I will send trustworthy help to him and your aunts. And if you want to bring out your sisters in London society, I will see that they have everything they need."

Instead of the smiles and thanks he expected, Meg's forehead crinkled in a frown.

He lurched on, afraid of the silence. Afraid she might speak and refuse him.

"I admit I am awkward speaking of emotions I never thought I possessed. I have no facile tongue off which the flowery phrases of the poet flow. For that I apologize and ask your indulgence."

She took the velvet box out of her reticule and set it on the edge of the fountain. "I am sorry. I cannot stay here at Wakefield with you, Nicholas." She jumped up and ran away from the fountain.

He stood in confusion for a moment, then noticed a party of ladies heading toward him on the path.

"Lord Wakefield," one called out.

He was trapped.

Meg held her skirts high and fled as fast as she could. If she had stayed another moment, if he had said one more thing about how he had changed his beliefs about love, if he had pulled her to him, if he had kissed her cheek, she would have reneged on her answer. She wanted to stay, she wanted to be near him always. But he had not mentioned love or marriage. Those were common words, common thoughts for a man who talked of caring for a woman. But she would not be a mistress. Never.

Panting, she veered off toward the villagers' celebration. She found Mr. Ames and his son watching the dancing under a string of brightly colored lanterns. He was a man she could trust.

"Can you find someone to drive me to a posting inn? I need to get home to Sussex?"

"When?"

"Right now. I need to get back to my father and my sisters," she pleaded.

After a long hesitation, he nodded. "Not many of the folks here are in any shape to harness up a rig and drive it, but I will find someone. I don't know what yer running from, Miss Hayward, but I never can figure out just what the fancy folks are up to. And I guess you got yer reasons."

"I just have a very scary suspicion that something has happened at home. It is a sort of premonition." Meg felt her lie was totally justified.

"I ken have a rig ready and I'll meet you at the orchard, if yer wantin' to keep your journey a secret. And I'll not take you to the inn neither. I'll see you all the way home if I have to ask the way to Bexhill from every man I meet."

"Oh, thank you, thank you, Mr. Ames."

Meg approached the house cautiously. Many guests enjoyed the beauties of the garden at night, and she avoided every one of them. Judging all the help to be out dancing, she entered through the silent kitchen and stole up the servants' stairs. Her room was dark and she dared not light a candle, so she pulled back the curtains to let in a bit of the bright moonlight. In the dimness, she changed from her lovely gown into one of the familiar old muslins. She hung the gown beside her riding habit and lingered a moment to fondle the soft velvet. She wished she could take it along, but would she not look a like a Gillray cartoon wearing it in her donkey cart? She stuffed her other gown and her nightrail into the shabby bag she had arrived with and took a handful of coins and tied them in her handkerchief. The rest she left for Livy.

She changed her slippers for her sturdy half-boots and closed the draperies. She found a tinderbox and lit a candle in order to write a note to her sister. She used the premonition excuse and encouraged Livy to stay at Wakefield until she wrote from Sussex. *Do not worry, darling sister. I hope you and Jonathan and Lady Fenton make swift plans for a wedding. Whatever I can do to help, I will.* She signed it, placed it on the pillow, then turned and left the room.

Fifteen

Meg knelt in the early-morning shade of the garden and pulled at weeds threatening to overwhelm the carrots. Since her return yesterday afternoon, she had satisfied herself that all was well at Cawthorn Manor. Her father had hugged her but did not seem aware she had been gone for any more than a day or two. Bea and Dorie pestered her for details about Livy's betrothal until, over breakfast, Meg said she had told them everything. They were not satisfied but they accompanied Aunt Alice to town that day, delivering fresh tarts and eggs to their customers along the way.

A greater contrast with Wakefield Hall Meg could not imagine. Last night for dinner, they sat at the table with only Molly, their serving maid, bringing the dishes from the kitchen, dishes mostly prepared by Aunt Alice and Bea. The meal was simple, and that morning she had breakfasted on porridge rather than choose from a sideboard crowded with a variety of meats, eggs, and buns.

Her room tucked under the eaves had only two small windows and no silken counterpane. But there was the familiar scent of the sea to inhale and the fresh breezes off the Channel and the distant sound of surf. And the worn but loving faces of her father and aunts, the eager youth of her sisters, for comfort.

She had been so confused about the Earl of Wakefield. Now that she was home in her familiar surroundings, doing simple things like cooking lemon custard early that morning and now pulling unwelcome botanical invaders from the ground, she could hardly believe she had spent months in a palace, painted two murals for the Dowager Countess of Wakefield, even carried on a dalliance of sorts with her handsome grandson. It all seemed an illusion, a figment of her imagination.

Except she had not imagined Nicholas Wadsworth, tenth Earl of Wakefield. At least she had not imagined the way she felt about him, the tingles when he had been near, the way her body felt all soft inside and the way her heart pounded and her face flushed. The funny urges she had to press herself to his chest, to wind her arms around his neck, to kiss his lips, his cheeks, his ears, things she had never imagined herself wanting to do.

Even here in the vegetable patch, wearing her old sunbonnet and with dirt seeping through her gloves to her fingers, she felt the exquisite pain, the wild mixture of elation and longing, desire and need, clutching at her.

"Hello. Is anyone home?"

When she heard his voice, it was as though her heart exploded. For a moment the emotion was so overwhelming, she could not stand.

"I am here in the garden." Her voice was barely a whisper.

"Meg? Is that you?"

She stripped off her gloves, got to her feet, and waved at the earl. Nothing prepared her for her joy at simply seeing him standing near the manor, Diamond Dust beside him.

"I am over here." She rushed toward him as the boy came from the stable to take his horse.

He hurried in her direction, and though she was more than breathless by the time they met, she wondered how she could keep from shouting out his name. He solved the problem by grabbing her in a great hug.

"What were you thinking, you mindless girl, running away in the middle of the night. I had a devil of a time finding you. Your sister is frightened, and everyone but Grandmama is astounded." His words came out in a jumble, but she didn't care.

She had never admitted it to herself, but when she ran, she knew he would come after her if he loved her. It was too much to dream of, to let see the light of day, but on that long, dark carriage trip, she sat alone with her thoughts, going over and over his words to discern their meaning for him.

Now he was here with her and she knew his feelings whether he could admit them or not. He might not want her as his countess, but at least she knew he loved her.

He kept her from trying to explain by kissing her so deeply and squeezing her so tightly, her feet lifted off the ground.

"What were you thinking?"

She answered with her own question. "How did you find out I left?"

"I worried the rest of the night. You did not explain why you would not take the earrings. I could not find you after you ran away. By yesterday morning I knew you must have tried to get home. It didn't take me long to find out that Mrs. Ames was missing her husband and son, that they had hurried off before the dance was over. She would not tell me more, but that was enough. I left as soon as I could wish good-bye to some of the guests and get away."

"What did the countess say?"

"She told me to get going. When I left her she was in tears, though I could not decide whether they were tears of joy over the sketch you left for her, or tears of disappointment that you ran away. She expects me to bring you back, of course."

"Oh?"

"As the new Countess of Wakefield."

"Me?" Her voice was a shrill squeak.

"I told you I wanted you to stay, that I would care for your family, that we could be together always."

Meg laughed and cried at the same time.

He brushed away her tears and kissed her damp cheeks. "You never answered me, and when you fled, I decided you would have no choice. I have made up my mind, and even if you have me in complete dislike, I shall have you for my wife."

"Your wife. Your wife?"

"Well, what else? You do not expect me to compromise your good name by some other kind of arrangement, do you?"

"Certainly not. I just wish you would have explained about the marriage part."

"Hah!" he exclaimed. "You are a wretched gel with a wicked disregard for my consequence. You *did* think I was trying to make you my mistress." He broke into laughter.

"You see, I did not—"

"I should turn you over my knee for thinking such a thing of me. Just because I have no skill at a flowery turn of phrase or the adept approach of a practiced rake, you interpret my words with the worst of all possible meanings. Why I am in love with a minx like you I shall never, never know."

"Love, Nicky?" She began to tease him back. "You said you did not believe in love of any kind."

"That was before I knew you well enough to doubt all manner of thoughts I considered rational and sane. For the past day and a half, I have seen myself well down the path toward Bedlam, a path upon which you have driven me, Miss Meg Hayward."

He smothered her response with another kiss.

"Margaret, do we have a guest?" Baron Cawthorn squinted at the two of them in a tight embrace.

Nicholas released her slowly.

Meg jumped back from him. "Why, yes, Papa, this is my, ah, friend, Nicholas Wadsworth, the Earl of Wakefield."

"Friend, eh?"

Nicholas covered his surprise at being interrupted by the grizzled visage of an elderly man dressed in a black swallowtail coat. Nick bowed. "Your servant, sir. I have the honor of requesting a moment of your time, if you can spare it."

Meg's father nodded and slowly moved off toward the house.

"Before I go to him," Nick said, "I have something for you. He pulled out the box he had been carrying for the last forty-eight hours and handed it to her.

Meg opened it immediately, having no idea what it might contain. With a cry of delight, she grabbed the fan and let the box fall to the ground. "You had it repaired. My Fontainebleau fan!"

He swept her into his arms again and squeezed her tight.

When she could catch her breath, she leaned against his chest. "I thought you threw it away after I tore it."

"I was never sure just which one was real and which one was the copy, you know."

She thumped his shoulder. "You, my lord, are a reprehensible cad."

"And you, my dearest, are a scheming minx. I think we make a perfect pair."

"So do I."